# HOWL

# HOWL

## BY KAREN HOOD-CADDY

**DUNDURN**
TORONTO

Editors: Allister Thompson / Sylvia McConnell
Design: Jesse Hooper
Printer: Webcom

**Library and Archives Canada Cataloguing in Publication**

Hood-Caddy, Karen, 1948-
    Howl / Karen Hood-Caddy.

ISBN 978-1-926607-25-2

    I. Title.

PS8565.O6514H69 2011          jC813'.54          C2011-900558-1

1    2    3    4    5          15    14    13    12    11

We acknowledge the support of the **Canada Council for the Arts** and the **Ontario Arts Council** for our publishing program. We also acknowledge the financial support of the **Government of Canada** through the **Canada Book Fund** and **Livres Canada Books**, and the **Government of Ontario** through the **Ontario Book Publishing Tax Credit** and the **Ontario Media Development Corporation**.

Care has been taken to trace the ownership of copyright material used in this book. The author and the publisher welcome any information enabling them to rectify any references or credits in subsequent editions.

*J. Kirk Howard, President*

Printed and bound in Canada.
www.dundurn.com

|  |  |  |
|---|---|---|
| Dundurn | Gazelle Book Services Limited | Dundurn |
| 3 Church Street, Suite 500 | White Cross Mills | 2250 Military Road |
| Toronto, Ontario, Canada | High Town, Lancaster, England | Tonawanda, NY |
| M5E 1M2 | LA1 4XS | U.S.A. 14150 |

*To my grandmother, Ruth Griffith*

# CHAPTER ONE

Robin sat on her bed, her ears stiff with listening. The doorbell pinged again. She could hear her father and sister greeting the new guests. There was a bluster of sound as everyone said their hellos, then the voices faded as the new group moved into the living room and joined the general hubbub of the party.

She slid her open palms along her slacks to dry them. She wished she didn't have to go down there, wished she didn't have to see their big, wet eyes, wished she didn't have to hear one more person say, "I'm sorry...."

But maybe they wouldn't talk that way today. After all, it was her birthday, her twelfth birthday. Time to stop acting like a baby.

The problem was, she *felt* like a baby. Even now she could feel tears pooling on the rims of her eyes. She mashed her lips together so they couldn't wobble and pushed the cuffs of her sleeves into her eyes to sop up the wetness. She was *not* going to cry.

"You'll get over it."

That's what people had been saying to her lately.

But they lied. She would *never* get over it. *Ever*.

The doorbell rang again. Relentless shifted her sixty pound Black Labrador body and eyed Robin impatiently.

"I know. You want to be down there saying hello to everyone."

Relentless shifted from one front paw to another, her gaze riveted on Robin.

"Go then."

Relentless furrowed her brows but didn't move.

"Can I take your coat?" Ari was asking someone.

Robin frowned. She hated it when her sister acted like the mom. *Who does she think she is?*

"Where's the birthday girl?" someone called up the stairs.

Robin froze. *Don't. Don't come up here!* She listened for sounds on the stairs but only heard talking, then a loud burst of laughter. She turned her head sharply, as if she'd been slapped. *How can they act like this? As if nothing happened?*

Seeking distraction, she let her eyes roam over the bedroom she shared with Ari. On her sister's night table, the glossy faces of women smiled from the front of a magazine. The headline beneath the faces said, THINNER THIGHS NOW! Beside the magazine was Ari's make-up case. The size of a workman's toolbox, it held creams and colours, brushes, and blushes. Ari, only fourteen, already knew that she wanted to be a model. Tall and skinny, she'd been play-acting the part for years.

Robin leaned back against her pillow. Her side of the room was covered with books and test tubes and microscopes, none of which she'd touched for months. She sighed. Once upon a time she'd had the idea of being a scientist or inventor. She'd even thought about becoming a vet like her father. But that was before.

In the "before" time, her dad used to bring home books from the animal clinic and explain medical terms and diseases. In the "before" time, she and her sister had used to get along. In the "before" time — Robin stopped herself. Her chest felt squishy remembering.

Relentless nudged Robin's hand with her snout.

"Soon," Robin said softly. *Why do I have to have this stupid party anyway? And why wasn't it planned on a weekend when Kaylie could come?* As it was, there were only going to be a bunch of boring relatives.

She stroked Relentless, touching the velvety fur just behind her ears. Then she slid her hand down to her dog's swollen underbelly. Leaning over until her cheek touched the side of her dog's body, she whispered, "Hello, little babies."

She wished her father wasn't so angry about Relentless being pregnant. Of course, he blamed her for leaving the gate open, which she had. She'd even seen the other dog, some sort of German Shepherd. She'd shooed it away, but by then, of course, it was too late. For weeks afterwards, she'd kept Relentless out of her father's sight. By the time he noticed the swelling in her dog's belly, Relentless's pregnancy was well established.

"Why didn't you tell me about seeing the other dog?" he'd shouted. "If I'd known early enough, I could have put an end to things."

What did he mean "put an end to things"? Did he mean kill them? Would he have done that?

He had looked at her sternly. "The last thing we need right now is more chaos. Don't we have enough to deal with?"

Robin sighed remembering his words. Even now, they landed on her chest like fists.

Hearing socked feet thumping up the stairs, Relentless banged her tail against the bed frame.

Squirm rushed into the room. Robin smiled at him. He smelled like buttery popcorn.

"Come on," he said, pulling her arm. "There's presents! Millions of them."

Robin tensed. He was wheezing. When she went downstairs, she'd better check to see if his inhaler was on top of the fridge where it was supposed to be.

She let Squirm lead her down the stairs. Relentless trotted behind them like a concerned nanny.

The living room was full of people and balloons. After saying hi to everyone, Robin searched for her father and saw him slouched in a chair, staring out the window, a red party hat askew on his head. She looked away. She hated it when he did his staring-into-space thing.

She looked over at the food table and saw Ari surrounded by a group of male cousins. How could anyone so annoying be so popular?

When Ari saw her, she tossed back her long blonde hair and came over. "About time you showed up."

Robin waved her arm in front of her face like a wind-shield wiper. As usual, Ari's perfume was overpowering. Squirm sneezed, then sneezed again.

"Nice dress," Ari said.

Robin looked down at her pants. She was in the middle of giving her sister her best scowl when she noticed the gold necklace. Their mother's. Robin wanted to yank it off her sister's neck. It was bad enough that Ari *looked* like their mom. To have her wearing their mother's stuff was just too much.

"Here comes the rhino," Ari said under her breath.

Robin turned to see her aunt's stumpy figure heading their way. She held a tray of drinks towards them.

"Be nice to each other, you two," Aunt Lizzie said. She kissed Robin on the cheek. "Have a pop, birthday girl."

When all three of them had chosen a drink, their aunt continued on, offering drinks to the others.

Robin watched as her sister wiped the top of her pop can on her sleeve. Ari washed or wiped off everything — even bananas.

Ari pulled the tab on the can and raised it to her mouth.

"Look out for the spider," Squirm said.

Ari swung her arm away. A hiss of pop sprayed out, some of it getting on her top. She wiped the droplets away then scrutinized the can. "Very funny."

Squirm convulsed with laughter. "You're such a *girl!*" He looked as if he was going to laugh again, but coughed instead. Then coughed again. His hand flew to his chest as he fought for air.

Moving quickly, Robin grabbed his puffer from the fridge and put it in his hand.

Squirm rushed into a corner, turning his back to the party as he squirted a dose of the inhalant into his mouth.

Robin's throat felt hot. "Dad told you not to wear perfume around Squirm." It was all she could do not to run upstairs and dump the perfume down the toilet.

Ari arched her pencilled eyebrow then moved a strand of hair from her cheek with long, perfectly manicured fingers. Her nails were painted bubble gum pink. Robin despised bubble gum pink.

Aunt Lizzie clapped her hands. "Attention. Attention everybody. We have a surprise."

Robin groaned.

Aunt Lizzie waved at Squirm. "Okay, Squirmy, bring it in."

Squirm exchanged a look with Robin. It bugged him when someone called him "Squirmy." Robin flicked her hand, as if swatting away a fly. Squirm nodded, pocketed his inhaler, and ran off. Within moments, he reappeared with a big yellow *papier mâché* piñata, shaped like a fish.

"I made it." He grinned at Robin. "It's full of Smarties."

"Wow." It had been a long time since she'd seen him grin like that.

Her uncle stood on a chair and hung the piñata from the ceiling. He gave Robin a broom then wrapped a scarf around her eyes. Suddenly, everything was black. Fear squiggled in her belly. Hands arrived on her shoulders and spun her around. She lurched and widened her stance. She wanted to tear off the blind-fold and run upstairs, but the thought of her brother's smile made her stay.

"Hit it, Robin! Smash it!" someone shouted.

Robin raised the broom and sliced it through the empty air.

"To the right. No, higher! Yeah! Hit it, there. No, *there!*"

Robin slashed the broom, trying to find something solid. She could hear her aunt talking in a lowered tone.

"She's taking it hard."

Robin swung the broom and edged nearer to the voices. Was her aunt talking about *her?*

"Twelve is awfully young for something so terrible to —" another voice said, hushed and confidential.

"And Squirmy's only ten. That's way too young to deal with death."

Robin hit out in various directions, pretending to be completely engrossed in finding the piñata. She waited for her aunt and friend to speak again. She didn't have to wait long.

"Ari seems to be handling it best of all."

"Well, she is fourteen. Fourteen going on eighteen, if you know what I mean."

"She's cool as a cucumber, that one."

"Oh, she's hurting, she's just better at covering it up. I can't imagine her living at Griff's."

"They're moving to Griff's? In Ontario? Isn't his mother a bit wacky?"

Robin stumbled and bumped into a table. The sharp corner stabbed into her hip. Her dad was moving them to their grandmother's? She lived in the middle of nowhere!

"From Winnipeg to the back woods — that's a bit much. But look at him. He's got to get out of this house. He's barely coping."

"It's the grief. Makes a person crazy."

Robin wobbled. She felt dizzy, like she was going to pass out. Her hip throbbed.

"But Griff! She's so eccentric…."

Robin stabbed the air. Didn't "eccentric" mean "crazy"?

"Gord's telling them tomorrow."

Tomorrow! Something hot and furious blasted through Robin's arm. She wouldn't go. They couldn't make her. She pulled her arms back and let the full force of her anger shoot into the broom. She grunted from the force. There was a smashing sound. Relentless barked, and Robin yanked off the blindfold.

Ari looked up at the shattered light fixture. "Way to go, Robs."

Robin collapsed back against the wall and stared at her brother. He had tilted his face up to watch the sparks that were jetting away from the broken light like fireworks.

His voice was full of awe. "Cool!"

Robin shut her eyes. It was the only way to make the entire room disappear.

# CHAPTER
# TWO

Robin hefted the last heavy box and carried it through the house. The sound of her footsteps echoed through the empty rooms. She could hardly believe this place used to be her home. The walls had strange, light-coloured squares on them where the pictures used to hang, and there were gashes in the carpet where the legs of the furniture had pushed big round indentations into the rug.

She heaved the box into the van, dug her way deep into the back and arranged a place for herself and Relentless. She crossed her arms tightly. It was stupid making them move. Beyond stupid. And why now? It was the beginning of March break, and all her friends were off doing fun stuff, but not her. Her entire holiday was going to be lost to packing, travelling, and unpacking.

"I know it's asking a lot of you kids," her father had said when he'd told them. "But I —"

A long, empty pause had followed. Robin had waited for Ari to protest. After all, Ari was the one with all the friends — friends she was either hanging out with or talking to on the phone. But she hadn't argued at all. She'd simply put her hand over her father's and said in a small, baby-like voice, "It's okay, Daddy."

But it *wasn't* okay! It was gross making them leave their house, their school, their friends. The old family cottage at Leech Lake was fun to visit in the summer, but to live there? With Griff? The last time they'd been, Griff had just shot a wild turkey and was trying to get them all to help pull the feathers off. Squirm had done it eagerly, but Ari had just about lost her lunch. Then there were the leeches. Robin shivered. And the new school. And the new kids she'd have to face.

Now, sitting in the van, the stupidity of the move seemed colossal. She should just get out of the car right now and take off. Kaylie had said she'd hide her in the family shed. Robin would have gone if she could have taken Relentless. But she couldn't exactly hide a dog! And there was no way she would ever give Relentless up. Her mother had given her the dog. They'd picked her out together from a mass of squirming puppies. The memory of that day cut into her before she could stop it. She dug her knuckles into her eye sockets in a vain attempt to push the tears back in. Then she tightened the muscles of her chest and back, pulling her arms and neck firmly into her body until she was rigid. Anything to stop the feelings.

The car door squeaked, and Squirm climbed into the front seat. Her father and Ari climbed in as well.

"Goodbye, caterpillars," Squirm crooned. "Goodbye, ladybugs. Goodbye, bumblebees."

His father leaned into him. "There are *lots* of insects at Leech Lake."

"How could we forget," Ari said. "I had mosquito bites and blackfly bites on every part of my body the last time I was there. Even in my ears!"

Their father carried on. "And there are ducks and loons and big animals too, like deer and moose — even bears sometimes. I used to track them when I was your age."

"Bears?" Squirm's voice rose, then fell. "I still wish we could stay here…."

Hearing the longing in his voice, Robin jammed in her ear buds and began scrolling through her playlists. The car started to back out of the driveway. She refused to look up.

"Wait!" Squirm cried. "Owlie! We forgot Owlie!"

Although Robin wouldn't have minded forgetting the old stuffed owl, she was surprised her father had. But then he was forgetting things all the time lately. Last week, he'd gone shopping and left his wallet at home, and a few weekends ago, he'd dressed to go to work on a Sunday.

"He's in the backyard," Squirm cried, just in case his dad needed reminding. Their father got out of the car and headed off around the house. Squirm leaned back towards Robin.

He kept his voice low. "What if she comes back?"

"Squirm —" Ari said. Her voice sounded hollow and tired. And very, very sad. Squirm strained further towards Robin. He whispered, "But what if, I mean, what if there was a mistake and she didn't really die, and she came to find us and —" His small face contorted.

Robin sat quietly looking at her brother. How could so many freckles get packed into such a small area? She reached out and moved her fingers through his reddish corkscrew curls. He needed a haircut. Their mother used to take him to a barber named Joe, but no one remembered where Joe worked.

Robin drew in a long breath. She knew she should say their mother was never coming back, but she couldn't get her tongue to say such a thing. Besides, Squirm knew that. "We gave the neighbours our new address, remember?"

Ari let out a hot, irritated breath. Squirm's face softened, and he turned in his seat.

Robin's door opened, and her father positioned the huge stuffed owl beside her. The owl was almost two feet tall and had fluffy white, tan, and black feathers and large yellow eyes. Robin was used to her father's stuffed animals. He had a friend who was a taxidermist, so there had been many over the years. But today she just didn't feel like having a gigantic dead thing staring at her. She slunk down in her seat. Just when she thought life sucked to the max, there was something that made it suck more.

On the highway, an endless line of grey concrete buildings spewed charcoal-coloured smoke into the blanket of smog that covered the city. *No wonder the air stinks*, Robin thought. It put a funny taste in her mouth too. Last year, when she'd been the president of her Environmental Club, she'd read about all the toxins people carried around in their bodies from pollution. *Why don't people stop it? Because they don't care, that's why*. She wasn't going to care either.

She let herself drift off to sleep. When she awoke, all she could see were farmers' fields. As they travelled towards Ontario, the fields became snowier, and soon there were huge hills of snow on either side of the road. Robin couldn't see over them, so she was forced to stare ahead at the long black highway that snaked through the white landscape. Where were they driving to, the Arctic?

A car passed them on the highway. Robin looked at the people inside. The dad was driving, and two kids were in the back. The mom was up front. The woman smiled at Robin as they went by. Robin turned away quickly.

She slept again and woke to the sound of ice pelting the car. The highway had narrowed, and the huge snowbanks on the sides seemed to press against them. Robin felt as if she couldn't breathe. Relentless made little whimpering noises in her sleep.

Ari called out, "Dinner time." She leaned into the back seat and held out a sandwich.

Robin ignored the offering. Ari was acting like the mom again.

Ari glared and pushed the sandwich towards her.

Robin made no move to take it. Ari slammed it down on Robin's jeans, and peanut butter squished out the sides. Relentless stared, her mouth watering. Robin opened the window and tossed the sandwich out. Relentless gave her a look of anguished disapproval.

"Dad! Robin threw her sandwich out the window."

"Robin!"

Robin pushed her head back into the seat and closed her eyes. She turned her music up so loud, it made her teeth buzz.

They drove all day, then another, stopping at fast food restaurants and one night at a rundown motel. Hour after hour, all Robin could see were snowy fields and bush. At some point during the second night, the car stopped. Robin opened her eyes to the glare of street-lights. They were driving through one of the little towns near the cottage.

In the summer, the town always looked festive, with lots of people wandering around eating ice cream cones. Now, as Robin looked at the dark store windows and empty streets, the town seemed desolate. Even hokey.

"It looks so *small*," Ari said.

"It *is* small," their father said, "compared to Winnipeg."

"There's where we got worms last time," Squirm said, pointing to a store that had a hand-written sign saying LIVE BAIT!

"Great," Ari said.

Robin was glad to hear the upset in Ari's voice. She wanted her sister to feel miserable. It would serve her right. Their father would have listened to Ari if she'd tried to convince him. Robin didn't have a doubt that the three of them could have handled things on their own. It wasn't rocket science to shop and cook. They didn't need some *eccentric* grandmother to help.

"There's the Chinese restaurant," their dad said.

Suddenly the town was gone and they were on the highway again. No one spoke for the next half hour as they continued to the lake.

Because of the snow-covered roads, it was more than an hour before they turned up a snowy lane. Branches scraped the sides of the car, and falling snow thudded on the roof. They went around a corner, and their father brought the car to a halt. The headlights flashed on a mountain of snow. It took Robin a few minutes to realize it wasn't a mountain she was staring at but the old farmhouse, covered with snow. Someone appeared on the porch, a black profile against the lit window.

Squirm yawned. "Who's that?"

"Griff." His father's voice was tired and irritated. "Grandma Griffith. You remember her."

Ari sighed. "It all looks so different."

"Of course it looks different. It's winter. We've always been here in summer," their father said.

"She looks old," Squirm said. "Do we *have* to live with her?"

"I told you, we'll be in the main house, the one you see, and Griff will be in the cabin by the water. You'll remember it when you see it in daylight. Just grab your overnight stuff. We'll take in the rest tomorrow. Bundle up. It's cold."

"Thirty below," Squirm said, reading the car's dashboard. "Wow. It's colder than Winnipeg!"

Their father got out of the car, and Squirm yawned and followed. Robin stared after them, unmoving. Her brother looked so little beside their father's towering height. Beside her on the seat, Relentless pulled herself to her feet and looked at Robin, waiting.

Ari yanked up her hood. "It's frigging freezing in here." She pushed open her door, got out and slammed it hard. Head down, she walked quickly towards the house.

Robin sat in the car feeling the cold creep under her clothes. Relentless whined, and Robin finally got out of the car. Darkness swallowed her. In the city, there were always lights; streetlights, car lights, even airplane lights. Here, it was blacker than black. She couldn't even see Relentless.

She walked towards the house, her feet making loud crunching sounds on the hard snow. The farmhouse was dim inside and smelled of damp.

Griff, her long white hair tied in a thick braid, stepped forward and gave Robin a hug. Robin stiffened.

Griff led the three of them up a narrow stairway. She guided Squirm into one small room and the girls into another. Ari threw her things down on the wider of the two beds.

Too tired to argue, Robin collapsed on the bed without taking her clothes off. She heard Relentless clunk down on the wood floor beside her. In a few minutes, Griff came in and tucked the covers under her chin. Her hands looked huge.

"It's going to be all right," Griff said quietly.

"No, it's not," Robin said and turned to the wall.

# CHAPTER
# THREE

Squirm pushed against Robin's shoulder. "Rawwwbinnn! Wake uuuuuuuup!"

Robin's eyes snapped open. She saw the old-fashioned wallpaper, realized where she was and groaned. Only moments before, in her dream, she'd been in her old house. It had seemed so real. She'd been with her mom and —

Squirm bounced on the bed. "You should see the snow. There's mountains of it! Let's go out and make a snowman."

Robin turned in her bed, yearning to return to her dream, to her old life. "Make it with Ari," she mumbled. Her mouth was dry, and it was hard to get her tongue to move.

"She's gone to town with Dad. We're supposed to go to Griff's cabin for breakfast." He tugged at her bedcovers, and Relentless barked.

Robin gripped the covers fiercely. "Leave me *alone*!"

The violence in her voice startled her, obliterating both her dream and any hopes she had of going back to sleep. Everything was ruined now. She thrust the blankets aside and stumbled towards the bathroom. She looked at herself in the mirror. Her hair was wild, zig-zagging in all directions. She tried to smooth it down, but there was no controlling it. There was no controlling anything.

When she returned to the bedroom a few moments later, Squirm was standing by the window in a column of sunlight. He looked like a lost little boy waiting for someone to find him. Robin went and stood behind him, and he leaned back into her.

"Sometimes I feel her," he said.

Robin tensed, tightening her body so the feelings could not rise. She squeezed her brother's shoulder and moved to the window.

A vast sea of snow was spread before her. Great gobs of it covered the trees, the fences, and barn.

"We have a whole other week till we have to go back to school," Squirm said.

Robin stared out at the endless whiteness. And what were they going to do, make snowmen day after day?

"Wow, look at the lake," Squirm said. The top of it was all silvery. "I think that's ice," he said, peering forward. "It's like a giant skating rink."

A prickly anxiety crept into Robin's body. She stared at the lake. Frozen or not, the very thought of water made her feel all wobbly inside. She sighed. There were so many things she was afraid of now. She was becoming a complete wuss.

"Do leeches freeze?"

"How would I know!"

"Remember that time you had one on your face? Did you ever freak! All you had to do was pick it off. You didn't have to scream like that."

Yeah, right, she thought. That was another reason to stay away from the water. The blood-sucking leeches!

Squirm jumped. "Hey, you know what? I bet we could *skate* on that ice! Want to? We could go for miles!"

He turned, ready to bound off, but Robin grabbed him. There was no way she was going out on the lake.

"Let's go find Griff first," she said, putting him off. "Get some breakfast."

As she expected, Squirm tore down the stairs. As usual, food was his favourite thing.

At the bottom of the stairs, they pulled on their coats and boots and went outside. Relentless ran ahead along the path, her tail whipping happily from side to side.

Robin looked over at the property across the field. Usually she couldn't see it, but now that it was winter and all the leaves were down, she could see the farmhouse and several mounds of snow near the house that looked like snow-covered trucks and tractors. A dog barked loudly, straining on its rope. She remembered her father saying something about a new family moving in there, but she didn't know anything about them.

Squirm led them along a shovelled path towards their grandmother's cabin. The snow was so high on either side of her that the tips of Robin's mittens brushed against it as she walked. She scooped up a handful and held it to her nostrils. The snow smelled fresh and clean, unlike snow in the city. She scrunched it into a ball and threw it at Squirm. He laughed and threw a snowball back. They pitched snowballs at each other until they were breathless.

They had just gotten back on the path when it forked. One way led to Griff's cabin, which was down near the water, and the other led to an old grey barn, which tilted to one side in the field. Squirm took the path to the barn. It was just like her brother to be heading in one direction and end up going in another.

As they walked, a black snowmobile charged out from the neighbour's property. The hair on Relentless's neck stood up like dozens of toothpicks. She started barking furiously as the snowmobile roared towards them. Both riders were wearing helmets with big plastic faceguards, so Robin could barely see their faces, but the driver was a big man and the passenger was a girl with a long yellow ponytail. Was she his daughter?

The snowmobile was heading right for them. Robin clutched Squirm, sure they were going to be hit. At the last moment, the machine swerved but continued to circle around them. Robin felt her shoulders tense as blue gas fumes billowed into the air. The snowmobile made smaller and smaller circles, and Robin felt as if a noose were being tightened around them. Squirm began to cough. Worried that he was going to have an asthma attack, Robin eased his face into the folds of her coat. She put her hands over her ears and started to count, something she sometimes did when she was afraid.

She heard yelling and opened her eyes. Griff was trudging towards them, waving her arms as she moved, her long braid of white hair bouncing on her shoulders. When the snowmobiler saw her, he turned and roared off.

"Idiot!" Griff said, gathering the kids in close.

Robin pulled away from the embrace. She didn't like people hugging her any more. Hugging softened her, and she needed to be hard, on the alert and have her guard up.

Squirm watched the snowmobile charge off. "Who was that?"

"Our crazy neighbour," Griff said. "Rick Big Shot, I mean, Kingshot. I think that was his daughter on the back. Couldn't tell. He's had a lot of floozies hanging around since he got divorced."

Squirm coughed again, and Griff patted his back as she stared at the retreating snowmobile. "If he thinks he can bamboozle me into selling this place, he's got another think coming." Her words made white puffs in the cold air. "Come on, let's get inside. This cold would freeze the devil himself."

The cabin was nestled at the base of some giant, snowy trees and looked much smaller than Robin remembered. On the verandah, snowshoes hung from nails, and in the middle of the door was a large white animal skull.

"Wow," Squirm said, touching it reverently. "Is that a deer head?"

"Yup." Griff pushed the driftwood door handle and led them inside. The smell of wood smoke and maple syrup rushed towards them.

Griff helped them hang their coats, then using her shirttail as an oven mitt, pulled a plate of pancakes out of the warming oven. She put a pot lid over top, placed it on a rough-hewn wooden table, and got out the utensils.

Robin looked around the room. The cabin wasn't very big, only one room, and part of the space was taken up by a four-poster bed covered with a bright multi-coloured quilt. Around the bed were fishing rods, an axe, and bundles of dried things hanging from the rafters. Herbs? Probably, Robin thought. She could smell lavender.

She let her eyes scan the walls, but they stopped suddenly on one item. A gun. She bit at the corner of her fingernail and brought her eyes back to her brother. She was hoping they would both roll their eyes at Griff's weirdness. After all, who else had a grandmother who owned a gun? But Squirm, as during other visits, was enchanted, moving around the room, touching various bone fragments, rock, and feathers. Then he looked up.

"Hey, you've got Owlie."

Griff smiled as she set out the plates. "Your dad brought him in last night. Now there's a story...."

*And I bet you're going to tell it*, Robin thought. What was it about old people and stories? Back in Winnipeg, their eighty-year-old neighbour, Mr. Talbot, used to corner her into listening to his stupid reminiscences. Who cared?

"Tell us," Squirm said. Robin wanted to strangle him.

Griff's eyes danced. "It was a long time ago now. When your dad was in engineering school."

Robin turned sharply to Griff. "Dad was never in engineering school." She looked at Squirm. Maybe

Griff was getting that strange forgetting disease. Alz-something.

"Oh, but he was. Just not for long. Not that there's anything wrong with engineering school, it was just that your dad didn't give a hoot about *things!* It was *animals* he cared about. But his dad, your granddad, rest his soul, wanted him to be an engineer, so that's what he studied. Until Owlie dropped out of the sky one day and came to the rescue."

Squirm smiled as Griff loaded pancakes onto three plates. "Really? He just dropped out of the sky?"

Griff poured hot chocolate into two cups and handed them around. "Yup! He'd been shot. We never found out who shot him, but still, he landed right on the ground in front of your dad, who, bless him, picked up the poor thing and nursed him back to life. Owlie must have had a few talks with your dad along the way, because the next thing I knew, your father had chucked engineering and signed up for vet school — which is what he *should* have done in the first place."

Squirm helped himself to some pancakes and sluiced maple syrup all over them.

Griff chuckled. "You're not having syrup with your pancakes, but pancakes with your syrup." She put a pancake on Robin's plate and continued. "Anyways, Owlie and your dad were such good friends that when Owlie died, I got him stuffed. I thought he'd be a good reminder."

Robin ate part of her pancake but left the rest. She wasn't hungry.

Griff nodded towards Owlie. "Maybe after lunch, we'll take him down to the barn and see if he can spook some of the ten thousand mice out there."

"Yeah — I'll bet Owlie is *great* at spooking mice."

Robin sat back and watched as Griff licked her thumb and index finger clean of syrup. How could any woman have hands so huge?

Squirm helped himself to more pancakes and reached for the syrup. He tilted the jug towards his mouth, pretending he was going to drink the whole thing, then laughed at himself, and poured the syrup over his pancakes. "This is the best maple syrup I ever ate."

"It's one of my better batches," Griff said.

His eyes widened. "You made this?"

"The trees made it," Griff said. "The trees right around this cabin. I just collected the sap and cooked it down."

"Can I make some?"

"Sure! We'll start as soon as the sap's running. Won't be long now. Spring's just around the corner."

Robin looked out the window. Not according to what she could see.

"Cool!"

Griff tossed her head back and laughed at Squirm's enthusiasm.

Robin stared at Griff. There were two teeth missing from the back of her grandmother's mouth. Gross. She turned away and began examining the cabin again. Dark eyes met hers. The eyes belonged to a woman in a large tea-brown photograph that hung on the far wall. The woman was dressed in a long, old-fashioned dress that had hundreds of buttons going all the way to her chin, and her hair was piled on the top of her head as they used to do in the old days. The woman seemed to be staring right at her.

"I'm skinning a deer out back," Griff said to Squirm. "You can help with that if you've got a mind to." She glanced at Robin. "It's not for everybody."

*You got that right*, Robin wanted to say. Would it be rude if she left?

Squirm swallowed a huge mouthful. "You kill it?"

Griff's brow furrowed. "Let's just say I was looking for food, and it offered to provide."

"Can I see?" Squirm said, licking his plate.

"Just let me have my tea," Griff said, going to the fridge. A moment later, she held up a milk carton and shook it. "Darn, it's empty."

"There's lots at the farmhouse," Squirm said. "I'll go get some." He ran to the door, grabbing his coat on the way. "Be right back."

Griff smiled at Robin. "I'm going to like having a grandson around."

Robin sipped her hot chocolate. Not knowing what to say, she stared at the photo of the woman.

"That's Emmeline," Griff said, following Robin's eyes. "Emmeline Pankhurst. The suffragette."

Robin looked at the fiery eyes in the photograph and tried to remember what a suffragette was.

"They're the ones who got the vote for women. Which, by the way, they had to fight tooth and nail to get. Emmeline here chained herself to the British parliament buildings. Got thrown in jail, went on a hunger strike

— the whole shebang. She almost died. But she wouldn't give up." Griff moved her eyes from the photograph to Robin. "According to one of my great- aunts, we're related to her in some distant sort of way."

Robin looked at Griff's beaming face and suppressed a yawn. As soon as Squirm came back, she was going to make her excuses and go.

Griff cleared the plates and started washing the dishes. Suddenly, she pulled her hands from the water. "Where is that boy?" She wiped her hands on a tea towel. "He wouldn't have gone out on the ice, would he?" Her eyes grabbed Robin's.

*If he's seen an animal out there or something else interesting, that's exactly the kind of thing he'd do*, Robin thought. Squirm was always getting caught up in the adventure of the moment.

"Didn't your dad tell him the ice wasn't safe?"

Robin's mind scrambled. "I don't know, I don't think so. Squirm said this morning he wanted to go skating and —" Suddenly her stomach felt as if it were full of jumping frogs.

Griff pulled on her boots. "You check the farmhouse. I'll go down to the lake and see what I can see. Holler if you find him."

Robin pulled on her jacket and walked quickly along the trodden path to the house. She told herself she'd find him examining some farm relic or ice for-mation. That was Squirm. But what if that wasn't the case this time? What if something bad had happened? If there was one realization the last year had cut into her awareness, it was that bad things not only *could* happen, they *did* happen. Even when you begged them not to.

She quickened her pace, and when she got to the house she pushed open the door and yelled his name. No answer. She kicked off her boots and took the stairs in sets of two. He'd already started decorating his room. There were pictures of spiders and bugs on the walls, and on the floor he'd lined up his teddy bear collection. Beside that was his ant farm. Even from the doorway, she could see the ants crawling inside the glass enclosure. They might have been crawling all over her skin the way they made her feel.

She was about to leave when she saw something yellow stuffed under Squirm's pillow. *Is that what I think it is?* She inched forward as if expecting the floor to give way beneath her. When she was close, she reached forward and touched it. Her chest swelled. It was one of her mother's old T-shirts.

She yearned to bring it to her face and smell it but stopped herself. She tensed her muscles as she knew how to do and pushed the shirt away. Then she saw the photograph. Her eyes sank down into her mother's face before she could stop them. Her body careened forward as if it might just be able to fall into the photograph and be with her mom. Her chest flooded with emotion and pain. She pushed the photo away and ran from the room.

Back at Griff's, she flew through the door. He'd be there, she was sure of it. He'd roll his eyes at her worry as he did every other time she got panicky about him. But the cabin was empty. She ran back outside. Where could he be? Chasing animals? She scanned the fields. He must be out there somewhere. She stepped off the hardened path and plunged into snow so deep, it was up to her armpits. She dragged herself back to the path, returned to Griff's and strapped on some snowshoes. Robin felt as if she were walking with each foot in a garbage can lid, but they kept her from sinking, so she went down near the lake. It was impossible with all the snow to tell where the waterline started, so she stayed well back. Relentless followed in her tracks.

She scanned the lake. To her immense relief, there was no sign of Squirm. She couldn't see Griff either. Where had they gone? Making sure she didn't go further out than she thought the shore was, she moved towards the point.

Snow pelted her face, but she trudged on. When she reached the point, she stopped and rotated her body one way and then the other, surveying the lake. Wait a minute. Something *was* out there. On the ice. The thin ice. Fear squeezed her chest, making it hard to breathe. Squinting, she strained forward. It was difficult to see through the blowing snow, but she could make out a figure. Squirm?

No, it was too short to be Squirm. Then it moved. It was a dog, a large black dog. It was running across the ice. Not wanting Relentless to follow suit, Robin turned. Relentless? She wasn't behind her.

Oh no! That was Relentless out there!

Stabbed with dread, she cupped her hands at the sides of her mouth and began shouting as loud as she could.

"Relentless! Come! Come here. *Now!*"

Relentless sniffed the ice, investigating some interesting smell, but made no move to return to Robin's side.

Robin yelled louder, making her voice sound really stern. "Relentless! Come! That's a bad dog. *A bad dog! Come!*"

A crack raced like jagged lightning across the ice. The crack went just to the left of Relentless's paws, and she looked up, alarmed. As she did, the ice caved in under her, and she plunged into the cold water.

Robin's hand flew to her mouth. "No!"

Relentless pawed the water, splashing helplessly as she tried to get her legs up on the ice, but the ice kept breaking, making the hole bigger. She tried over and over to get a grip, howling every time she splashed back into the freezing water.

On shore, Robin paced furiously. Relentless was drowning! Drowning! She had to *do* something. And do something fast. But what? If she went out on the ice herself, she'd fall through too! Then she would drown. Blood pounded in her chest. She felt as if she were going to explode. Never had she been so afraid.

She dropped her face into her cold mittens. The nuggets of ice on the wool bit into her face, but she didn't care. The memory had come for her. And when it did, everything else disappeared.

She was in the water, sinking, helplessly sinking, going down. And down. And down. Her lungs screamed for air. She gulped and sputtered as she tried to claw her way to the surface, but her body was falling through the water as heavy as a stone. Water gushed into her nose and mouth. Then all became black.

# CHAPTER FOUR

A hand grabbed her and pulled her up. A huge hand.

"Griff!" Robin panted. "Relentless! She fell through the ice, she —"

"So that's what all the yowling's about!"

Robin pointed through the blizzard, and Griff strained forward. "Right you are. Let's just hope Squirm wasn't out there with her."

Robin stared at Griff, paralyzed by the thought.

Griff began to stride off. "Come on. Let's get some rope."

Robin's legs wouldn't move. Was Griff going to make her go on the ice?

Griff turned and put her big hands on Robin's shoulders. Her face was so close, Robin could feel the warmth of her grandmother's breath on her cheek.

"I know you're afraid," Griff said. "But help anyways. I can't pull the dog out by myself." She bounded away, yanking the rope she used as a clothesline as she went.

Robin chased after her, teeth chattering. "But what, what if you go in too?"

"Just hold the rope," Griff said firmly. "I'll take care of the rest." She wrapped the rope once, then twice around her own waist. She coiled the other end around Robin and positioned her behind a rock on the shore. Robin could hear Relentless howling in the background.

"Lean against the rock and hold on tight!"

"But what if I can't?" Robin cried. Her face was hot and wet, and she smeared her coat sleeve across it. If Griff fell in, and she let go of the rope, Griff would die too!

Griff's eyes bored into hers. "You can do this. I know you can."

Robin crunched down and pressed her body as hard as she could into the rock. When she felt she was in the strongest position she could manage, she peeked over the top of the rock and watched as Griff lay down, splaying her arms and legs wide to spread out her weight, and began to inch out onto the ice.

Relentless was several feet away and still thrashing, but in a slow, exhausted way. She had sunk deeper into the black hole, and now the freezing water was just below her ears.

Robin gripped the rope as tight as she could and leaned back, tensing her whole body so she'd be prepared if there was a sudden tug. Her jacket had ridden up, and the snow was biting into her skin just above her pant waist. The coldness of it hurt like crazy, but she knew she couldn't let go of the rope to pull her coat down, even for a second.

She could hear Griff talking to Relentless.

"I'm coming, sweetheart. Don't you worry. I'll be there any minute now. Don't you go drowning on me. That's a good girl."

Slowly, very slowly, moving centimeter by centimeter, Griff neared the hole in the ice. Robin knew that this was where the ice would be thinnest. This was where another hunk of it could break off, plunging her grandmother into the deathly cold water. Robin would have to watch both of them die. And it would all be her fault.

"Tighten the rope!" Griff shouted.

Robin heaved herself to standing and yanked her body to make the rope even more taut. Then she braced her snowshoes on the rock for support. Every cell in her body was screaming. *Hold on. Please.*

Snow lashed her face. The snow was so dense, she couldn't see Griff any more, so she closed her eyes and started counting. When she'd counted to sixty, she started all over again. She was at thirty-five when she heard a loud crack. Had Griff fallen in? She felt something warm and wet trickle between her legs. She couldn't have stopped the pee if she'd tried.

The snow let up for a moment, and Robin strained to see what had happened. To her huge relief, she saw her grandmother still lying face down on the ice, almost right beside the hole now. Robin bit her lip as she watched Griff reach out with her hand. Robin closed her eyes but opened them again just as Griff grabbed the dog's collar. In one huge tug, Griff pulled Relentless out.

A loud cheer whooped from Robin's mouth.

Relentless yelped and leapt into the air happily, as if it had all been a game.

Griff edged herself back to solid ground and stiffly pulled herself to standing. Relentless came bounding towards her. The dog shook, spraying ice water all over her.

"You're welcome." Griff grinned and began gathering up the rope.

Robin fell to her knees and hugged her dog. Relentless licked her face with her warm tongue.

"I'd lick your face too if I were a dog," Griff said. "You were very brave."

Robin shook her head. She hadn't been brave at all. In fact, she'd been so scared, she'd peed in her pants. It didn't get much worse than that.

"It's easy to do brave things when you aren't scared. But you *were* scared. That's courage, my girl. Real courage." Griff hugged her hard.

Robin went rigid. She couldn't, wouldn't, let her grandmother comfort her. She'd been a wuss. A complete wuss.

# CHAPTER
# FIVE

The wind pushed against them as they trekked back to Griff's cabin. Robin had to tuck her head down and lean forward to make any progress. She had taken off the snowshoes, but her pee-soaked pants had stiffened in the cold and it was difficult to walk, but she didn't care. Relentless was wagging her tail at her side. Now all they had to do was find Squirm.

"Must be all this global warming," Griff said. "The lake isn't freezing like it did in the old days. Used to be you could drive a truck across it all winter long. Now, seems like every year some bozo on a snowmobile breaks through and drowns. Even in the dead of winter. But heavens, it's almost the end of March. It's never safe this time of year. Anyways, I'm telling you all this 'cause I want you to know that being scared of going through the ice is nothing to be ashamed about. In fact, it's kind of smart."

"It's not just ice, it's —" Robin felt her throat swell, and no other words could get through.

"The water? You're afraid of water? Is that what you're saying? But the last time you were here, my goodness, you swam like a fish! What happened?"

Robin's throat hurt. There was no way she could talk.

Griff was quiet. "Everyone gets afraid sometimes. Even me. Maybe in the summer, you and I can go into the water together. Swimming's too lovely a thing to miss out on."

Robin's shame gagged her into silence. Lately, fear seemed to be tying her up like a hostage more and more.

"Relentless can teach you to dog paddle," Griff said. "Did you know that Black Labs were bred for cold water? That's why they have webbed feet. And such thick fur. They were bred to rescue sailors who went overboard."

At the cabin now, Griff pushed open the door to let Robin go in first. "I'll get you something to change into."

Squirm rushed towards them. "Where were you guys? I've been waiting here for ages!"

"Looking for you, to start with," Griff said.

"Sorry," Squirm said. "When I went to get the milk, I saw a deer and chased him for a bit." He looked at Griff apologetically. "Milk's in the fridge."

Griff passed Robin some flannel pajama bottoms as Relentless plunked herself down beside Squirm.

"Hey, how come she's so wet? She's sopping."

Robin moved to the other end of the cabin to change and let Griff explain.

"She went for a swim." Griff knelt beside Relentless and began towelling her down. "You two sure gave this dog the right name. She *is* relentless." When the towel had absorbed as much water as it could, she put it aside and handed Squirm a dry one. "She just didn't give up, did you, girl?"

As Squirm rubbed Relentless with the towel, Griff stoked the woodstove. "Goodness, that tuckered me right out. I need some sustenance." She heated up some soup and when it was ready, the three of them sipped it out of mugs and ate crackers from a box as they sat on the floor.

Squirm handed a cracker to Relentless, but she turned her head away. Squirm looked grim. "What's the matter, girl, aren't you hungry?"

Relentless started to pant.

Robin's eyes flew to Griff. "How come she's breathing like that?"

The skin on Griff's face became as wrinkled as a brown paper lunch bag. She let out a long breath. "I think she's going to have her puppies!"

Squirm's eyes widened. "Right now? But they're not supposed to come yet."

"All that cold water's probably throwing her into an early labour." The lines on Griff's face deepened.

Robin's stomach churned with anxiety. "Will the puppies be okay?"

"I don't know," Griff said, walking towards the phone. "I think we'd better call your father. What's your dad's cell number?"

Robin called it out. "But he never has it on."

After letting it ring for a long time, Griff turned to Squirm. "Go up to the house, will you? And leave your dad a note. Tell him to come the second he gets home."

Squirm ran out, and Griff began boiling water and assembling towels. They made a makeshift bed for Relentless and coaxed her onto it.

Squirm came back in, snowflakes covering his head.

"Is it ever snowing out there!" He sat down beside them. "So, how come Relentless went swimming?"

Griff told Squirm about Relentless falling through the ice and how she and Robin had pulled the dog out.

"Weren't you scared?" Squirm asked, looking from one to the other.

Griff swatted the air. "A bit. But I was roped to Robin — I knew I was safe." She smiled at Robin and rubbed the dog's back. Relentless kept changing her position, as if she couldn't get comfortable. She started panting again.

"It's okay, girl. It's okay," Robin whispered over and over, but what if it wasn't?

Hours passed as they hovered around the distressed dog.

"Look at how swollen her vulva is," Griff finally said.

Robin had heard the word "vulva" before but wasn't sure what it did or where it was, but she could see an area near the dog's tail which was pink and bulging.

"I'd say those puppies are coming through any moment."

"But what if it's too soon?" Robin asked.

Griff patted her face gently. "Just leave the 'what ifs' out for now, okay? They'll make us both worry."

Robin blushed. She hated being reprimanded.

Squirm pointed to the dog's tail. "Oh, no — look, she's having a poo."

A dark mass ballooned out of a small opening at Relentless's rear.

"That's a puppy," Griff said. "That's how they come out, wrapped in a little bag."

Relentless began licking the outside skin on the pouch then nipped it with her teeth. It tore like cling-wrap and she was able to lick off the rest of the covering. Inside was a tiny baby dog. It was only a few inches long and had a pink head and four pink paws. Its eyes were closed, and it was making barely audible mewing sounds and moving its head in a wobbly, drunken kind of way.

Squirm pointed to the string attaching the puppy to Relentless. "What's that?"

"The umbilical cord," Griff said, smiling. "You had one attached to your mom too, but the doctor cut it off." Relentless quickly chewed through the cord. "He just doesn't do it with his teeth like Relentless!" Squirm laughed, and Griff arranged the tiny puppy so it was close to one of Relentless's nipples. The puppy made a deep, guttural sound as it began to suck. "I thought that's what this little fellow was looking for."

The new puppy suckled for a few moments then nodded off, asleep at the task. A while later, a second bulge appeared, and soon another puppy was deposited on the bed of towels. "Here, Robin, you hold the first one, and I'll take care of the second." Griff lifted the first puppy and put it on a towel in Robin's lap.

Robin felt a rush of air go into her lungs as she held the puppy. She felt almost weightless, as if she'd suddenly been filled with a dozen coloured balloons and might simply float off the ground. She stared at the puppy. Never had she seen anything so tiny and adorable. Could something that small live?

When the third puppy started to arrive, Griff gave the second one to Squirm.

"Wow," he said in a quiet, awed voice. He cradled it and stroked it gently with the tip of his finger.

Over the next few hours, Relentless delivered four more babies. More time passed, and they waited for the rest of the puppies to arrive. None came.

"I just know there are more in there," Griff said as she stroked the dog,

Relentless began to whine and whimper.

Robin looked at Griff. The deep lines on her grandmother's face seemed to be all tangled up.

"Is she going to be okay?" Robin asked.

"I'd like to say yes, but I really don't know," Griff said. "The poor thing is utterly exhausted."

Robin winced. When her mom had been sick, everyone always said she was going to get better. When she didn't, Robin had felt utterly betrayed. But now, for the first time, she understood why people had said what they did. Sometimes the truth was just too hard to bear. Yet still, she was glad Griff had told her the truth.

"Sure wish Dad would get here," Squirm said as they waited.

It seemed to Robin as if hours had passed when there was a sudden burst of cold air and the sound of a door shutting.

Robin and Squirm shouted at the same time. "Dad!"

Griff's hand flew to her heart. "Gordon, thank goodness you're here."

He strode in, Squirm's note still in his hand. Ari, who was behind him, took a few tentative steps towards them.

"Puppies!" Elated, Ari sat down and Griff put one of the puppies in her arms. Her face softened with joy.

Their dad pulled out his stethoscope and listened to Relentless's heart. Then he probed her belly.

"She fell in the lake," Robin said.

He yanked the stethoscope from his ears and began pulling things from his bag. "We've got to get the rest of the puppies out of there."

Robin watched him fill a syringe and inject it into her dog's leg. Relentless went limp immediately.

Her father put his hand on Robin's arm. "It's okay. She'll wake up in a little while. Right now, I need to open her up and get the other puppies out."

"You can do that?" Squirm asked.

"Like pulling apples out of a bag," he said as he put on some plastic gloves. He did a quick prep of the dog's abdomen. "Can you hold her in position?"

Robin helped Griff ease Relentless on her back, then watched as her dad made a long incision into the dog's belly with his scalpel. Squirm gasped, and Ari put the dog she was holding into Robin's lap then went back to the farmhouse. Robin, however, watched in fascination as her father blotted up the blood then eased the skin on either side of the incision apart. With the dog's innards exposed, he reached in and pulled out what looked like a long sack. With his scalpel, he cut into the bag and extracted a puppy.

"Wow!" Robin whispered.

Her father snipped the umbilical cord then took a plastic instrument and suctioned out the puppy's nose. Smiling now, he passed the puppy to Griff.

"Give it a good rub with the towel," he instructed. "We want to replicate what Relentless would have done with her tongue. That will get everything working!"

Griff massaged the new puppy, but it showed no signs of life.

"Rub harder," he instructed.

"I'm scared of being too hard," Griff said, but she rubbed more vigorously. "Come on, little one. Your life is waiting for you out here. There's a lake, woods, and skunks to chase. Come on, take a breath!"

"It's moving, look!" Squirm cried.

His dad nodded, but he was concentrating on pulling out another puppy. When he'd cleaned this one up, he passed it to Robin. She received it like a holy thing. These puppies were the most precious things she'd ever touched. Griff helped her rub it into life.

Squirm got the next puppy and began massaging it the moment it was placed in his lap. When the puppy did not move, Griff took over, massaging it as strongly as she dared. Then their dad tried. After a few moments, he shook his head.

"I'm afraid this one isn't going to make it."

Squirm looked up at him, alarmed. "It's dead?"

His father nodded gravely and turned to deliver the next puppy.

Neither of the next two puppies could be brought to life. Their dad put a towel over the three inert bodies.

"Oh well," Griff said. "We saved most of them." She gave her son a weak smile. "That's more than we would have saved if you hadn't shown up." She touched his arm gratefully.

Robin wanted to get up and hug her dad, but she didn't.

Soon he yawned and stood. "I'm going to get some formula for the puppies."

"Can't she feed them?" Robin asked.

"She doesn't have enough teats," he said. "But also, she'll recover faster if we supplement." He brought in small feeding bottles and filled each one with formula. Robin set one of the tiny puppies in the crook of her arm. Its eyes were closed and its whole body throbbed every time its heart beat. Gently, she eased the nipple of the small bottle into the puppy's mouth and smiled as it made little grunting noises and began to suck. A warm happiness spread through her, a happiness she hadn't felt for a long time.

Her father started packing up his bag. "These puppies are going to be a lot of work." He looked at Robin and frowned. "They'll need feeding every four hours. That means someone will have to get up at two or three in the morning and again at dawn."

"I'll take the night shift," Griff said.

Robin turned to Squirm. "And we can share the early morning one."

Squirm nodded quickly. "Hey — if we sleep here, we can feed them in the morning, then go right back to sleep." He looked from his father to Griff. "Can we?"

"I don't see why not," Griff said. "That way, you'll hear them hollering...."

"We'll move them out to the barn when they're a bit older," their father said.

Griff looked at her son fondly. "Remember all the animals you used to keep out there?" She looked at her grandchildren. "Your father used to take in every stray animal that came his way."

He suppressed a smile. "Don't give them ideas." He looked at Robin and Squirm. "The last thing I want is a bunch of animals at home to take care of. I have enough at the clinic. But these won't be here for long. In a few weeks we can find homes for them."

Did he mean Relentless, too? Robin didn't think so but didn't want to ask. It was never a good thing to ask her father anything when he was tired.

Her father went back to the farmhouse, and Squirm followed to get his puffer. Robin lay down on the floor. She felt so sleepy, she could hardly keep her eyes open.

"Good idea," Griff said, lying down beside her. "I'm whacked right out."

Robin smiled. She could hear the puppies making little grunting sounds and feel the heat from the back of Griff's hand that was touching hers. It felt as warm as a stone in the sun.

"I know you're tired," Griff said, "but I need to say something. Can you hear me out?"

Robin opened her eyes and tried to concentrate.

"It may not be something you understand now, it may not be something you understand ever, but I've got to say it anyways."

Robin suppressed a yawn.

"What I want to say is this," Griff began. "Life can be brutal. It can rip things away from you, even rip away people, people we love." She squeezed Robin's hand then let it go. "But I want you to remember that it can also give, give good things like puppies and well, all kinds of other things that you're going to experience. So don't go thinking that life isn't good. It *is* good. At least it can be. Very, very good. Don't let yourself close down to that, okay?"

Robin tucked Griff's words into her memory so she could think about them later then let the fuzzy blanket of sleep pull itself over her mind.

# CHAPTER
# SIX

For the rest of the March holiday, Robin did nothing but feed the puppies, play with the puppies, and help Relentless heal from the surgery. She still had her stitches in but was recovering well, and Robin believed her father's assurances that soon she would be her old healthy self.

After the birth of the puppies, Robin had stayed at Griff's most of the time. Then, suddenly, it was the night before the new spring term at school, so she reluctantly moved back to the room she shared with Ari. The boxes of her stuff from their old house were still piled at the end of her bed.

Ari, whose side of the room was box-free and immaculate, was laying out her outfit for the next day at school.

"When are you going to unpack your stupid boxes?" Ari demanded.

Robin shrugged and didn't answer. Sometimes it felt good to get her sister mad.

"Your side of the room is a pigsty!"

"Are you calling me a pig?" Robin knew it was dangerous to taunt her sister, but she couldn't stop herself.

"Oink, oink," Ari said.

Robin ignored her and began rummaging through one of the boxes in search of something for school. Not that she really cared. She picked out a pair of clean jeans and her favourite apple-green top, the one her mother had given her.

Ari got out her nightdress and took off her clothes. Whenever Robin changed, she always turned away from her sister, shy about being naked. Ari, however, always seemed glad to show off her body.

Robin tried not to stare, but she couldn't help herself. Her sister had breasts now, and every time Robin saw them, they were fuller and bigger. Robin wondered whether she would have breasts that big. She wanted them and didn't want them, all at the same time.

She turned away, got into some flannel pajamas and climbed into bed. It felt strange not to be snuggling up with Relentless and the puppies. Feeling unsettled and agitated, she turned towards the wall and tried to get comfortable. Soon she could hear the rhythmic sound of her sister's breathing.

Robin couldn't get herself to relax. She kept thinking about the next day. What if the kids were mean? What if she didn't like her teacher? What if she said something stupid or didn't know the answer to a question? Her father had told her at dinner that he thought she'd find it easier to make friends in a small school. Robin might have agreed if it had been at the beginning of the school year, but it wasn't. At this point in time, she was going to stick out like a sore thumb. Everyone would know she was new, and they'd stare at her. She *hated* being stared at. This was a situation where she wouldn't have minded having Ari along — no one ever looked at Robin when Ari was around. But Ari was in grade nine now and would be going to the high school.

At least she didn't have to worry about getting there; Griff had said she was going to drive them. Did that mean she was going to introduce them to their new teachers? Something went "glunk" deep in Robin's gut. What if Griff laughed, and everyone saw her missing teeth? Robin's eyes stung as if the humiliation were happening at that moment.

If only she could get to sleep. She counted sheep, she counted ice cream cones, she counted puppies, but nothing seemed to help. The next thing she knew, the high-pitched sound of a hair dryer was blasting her awake. What was Ari doing drying her hair in the middle of the night? She opened her eyes, saw the daylight, and pulled the covers over her head. The smell of coconut hair gel filled her nostrils anyway.

"Oink, oink. Time to get up."

Robin didn't move. Suddenly, the covers were ripped off her bed.

"Hey!" Robin scrambled to pull them back. The room was freezing. She took a quick glance at the clock. Seven thirty? No! It couldn't be! She'd wanted to get up early so she could feed the puppies. She jumped up and threw on some old clothes. She'd dress for school when she got back.

She ran to Griff's and yanked open the door. Relentless came towards her, wiggling with excitement.

"Careful, girl. Your stitches —"

"Oh, she's healed up now. Tighter than a drum," Griff said. "Your dad told me he's taking out the stitches any day now." She was sitting quietly in a chair, a heap of puppies in her lap.

Robin nuzzled into Relentless, grateful she was nearly all healed. "Sorry I'm late."

"Not to worry," Griff said. "Between Relentless and me, they're all fed now. Greedy little blighters. Have you seen how much they've grown in a week?" She grinned at Robin. "They'll be opening their eyes any time now."

Robin groaned. She didn't want to miss that. "Do I *have* to go to school?"

Griff waved her off. "Go, get ready. I'll be up in a few minutes to drive you."

Robin went back to the house, changed and went down to the kitchen.

"Dad went to see a sick cow," Squirm said as he slurped the milk from his cereal bowl. His spoon clattered to the floor. He picked it up and wiped it on his sweater.

"Wash it," Ari ordered.

Squirm licked the spoon. "Yum. Germs!" He grinned and looked at Robin.

"Okay, get sick. See if I care," Ari said, pushing the cereal box Robin's way.

Robin looked at the clock. If she were back in her old life, she'd be meeting Kaylie right now. They'd be laughing and talking as they walked to school. Listlessly, she ate a few handfuls of dry cereal. Then she heard Griff honking, and the three of them gathered their things.

Seeing the pick-up truck with its big old-fashioned fenders, Ari rolled her eyes. "We actually have to get in that junk heap?"

The passenger door swung open and Squirm climbed in. "Cool!"

When they were all in the car, Griff yanked the green tennis ball that was taped to the top of the shift stick. There was a loud, grinding sound as she put the car in gear. They drove down the rutted lane, the four of them jostling against each other and sometimes up into the car roof. The drive got smoother when they reached the main road.

"Goodness, this is the first time since December the road's got no snow on it. Spring must be on its way."

They drove into town, stopping to drop off Ari at the high school. When they arrived at the public school Robin and Squirm would be attending, Griff handed them both a brown paper bag.

"Lunch. Pick you up here when school's out. Tomorrow you'll go by bus."

Squirm looked at the school doubtfully. "But where do we go?"

"Oh, right." Griff reached into her pocket for a wrinkled piece of paper. "Squirm, you're in Ms. Robinson's, room 212, and Robin, you have Mr. Lynch, room 315."

So much for Griff trying to play "mom," Robin thought as she walked Squirm to his room. Just as he went in, the bell rang. Great. Now she was going to be late for her own class, and everyone would stare at her as she walked in.

She found her classroom and hesitated at the doorway. A tall, thin teacher waved her forward.

"You must be Robin Green." Mr. Lynch motioned to a seat at the front beside a girl who had glasses as big as water goggles.

Robin nodded and slunk into the vacant seat. She didn't see the two books on the desk top. They made a loud "fwap" when they hit the floor.

"Klutz," someone said. Kids snickered.

The teacher looked up, his voice full of warning. "Brittany —" He turned and started writing on the blackboard.

The girl in front of Robin turned in her chair. "Hi, I'm Zoey. But everyone calls me Zo-Zo." She lowered her voice. "Don't worry about Big Brat, I mean Brittany. She's mean to everyone."

Robin kept her eyes down. If that was supposed to make her feel better, it didn't.

Mr. Lynch faced the class and began explaining what to expect in the term ahead. Robin had to force herself to pay attention. Usually, she would rivet her eyes on the teacher and take notes, no matter how inconsequential, but that was before. When things mattered. This year was going to be different. This year there was going to be no putting her hand up all the time, no being the star student. No extra stuff either like heading up the environmental club as she'd done at her previous school. Why should she? Where had it gotten her? Bad things *still* happened.

Halfway through the morning, Mr. Lynch told the class he was going to put them in pairs for a Social Studies project.

Robin groaned. What if she got partnered with Brittany?

"Okay, class, I'll read out the topics," Mr. Lynch said, "and you can put up your hand for the one you want." He looked at Zo-Zo. "Zoey, will you write down who's interested in what?"

Zo-Zo pulled out a notebook and clicked her pen in readiness.

Robin stared at the girl. She looked like the female counterpart to her brother Squirm with her small frame and freckles. But Zo-Zo's hair was brown, not red, and she wore glasses. Huge ones.

"Some of the topics are environmental," Mr. Lynch said. "And speaking of that, this year we have a student who's won awards for her environmental work." He unfurled his arm like a red carpet towards Robin.

Robin felt heat as blood rushed to her face.

"Now, Robin, since you don't know anyone, I'm going to pair you with —" he scanned the class, "Brodie. Put your hand up, Brodie, so she knows who you are."

Robin turned. Her stomach did a flip. A boy with a kind, lean face and the biggest, brownest eyes she'd ever seen smiled at her.

Zo-Zo leaned towards Robin. "Lucky you," she whispered. "Brodie's cool."

He certainly looked cool, Robin thought. Something light and airy went through her chest. Maybe this school was going to be all right after all.

Then she felt something crawling on her skin. It wasn't an insect, but someone's glare.

Robin shifted her glance and noticed the blonde girl behind Brodie giving her a mean, hateful look. The girl was large, not fat but big-boned, and her face was splotchy with anger.

Robin turned away. What was the girl's problem?

"That's Brodie's super-sized girlfriend, Brittany," Zo-Zo said as she flicked one of her long brown braids behind her. "She's *not* cool. She thinks she *owns* Brodie."

Mr. Lynch frowned at Zo-Zo for talking, then said, "Brodie, Robin, your assignment is to design a game to make the school more environmentally friendly."

Robin bit her nail. Just what she needed, another environmental project that made no difference to anything.

Mr. Lynch paired the rest of the class and gave out assignments. When he was finished, he moved to the blackboard.

Zo-Zo waved her hand. "What about me, Mr. Lynch? You didn't pair me up with anyone. Can I go with Brodie and Robin?"

"Sure," he said, just as the bell rang for lunch.

Zo-Zo came and stood beside Robin's desk. "Wow — an environmental hero!"

Robin stopped chewing on her nail. "It was no big deal." All she had done was organize a paperless lunch campaign at her old school. Most of the job had been hounding people to bring their lunches in reusable containers. The problem was, the moment she'd stopped hounding them, they went back to their old ways. The whole thing had been a complete waste of time.

Zo-Zo stared at her. "Big Brat will really hate you now."

Robin snuck a glance across the room. Brittany had gathered her books and was waiting for Brodie, who didn't seem in any hurry to join her.

Zo-Zo tapped her pen against her lips. "The Kingshots act like they own everything."

"Kingshots? My neighbour is Rick Kingshot."

"That's Brittany's dad," Zo-Zo said, raising her eyes to the heavens. "Whoa. Random. I wouldn't want Brittany as *my* neighbour. It's bad enough being in the same class. But her brother's sort of cool. Good-looking, anyway. Conner. My sister's got a thing for him. She says all the girls in high school do."

Robin stared at Zo-Zo. Brittany must have been the girl on the back of the snowmobile the other day. Robin tried to swallow, but her throat was too dry.

"Rick Kingshot is running for mayor. My dad says if the guy wins, he's going to shoot himself." Zo-Zo pulled a digital camera from her desk. "And now you're his neighbour. I've got to put this in my column." She snapped Robin's picture before Robin could stop her. "I have a column in the *Cottage Country News*! My dad's the editor. I'll put it on my blog too. It's called 'Kids Biz.' Check it out." She slipped the camera back into her backpack and led Robin into the cafeteria.

They stood in the food line. Brittany and Brodie were a few people ahead of them. Robin watched as Brittany blew large gum bubbles into Brodie's neck.

Brodie pulled away every time Brittany lunged towards him, but he was laughing.

"Brittany's only at her dad's on weekends," Zo-Zo said. "So at least you won't have to put up with her *all* the time. She stays with her mom during the week." She sighed. "I wish I could stay with *my* mom."

Robin wondered whether to ask Zo-Zo where her mom was. But what if Zo-Zo then asked about *her* mom?

"My mom lives in another town," Zo-Zo said. "I don't get to see her much."

At least you can visit her, Robin thought. Or phone her. She'd amputate a hand to be able to do either of those things.

The line moved slowly, and Robin kept finding herself staring at Brodie. Then Brittany caught her looking at him and gave her another nasty look.

"Be careful," Zo-Zo warned. "She's got a mean streak. So does her brother, Conner. Someone told me he kills raccoons just to get their tails."

Robin pulled her eyes away and began examining the various lunch options behind the counter.

"I'm getting fries," Zo-Zo said, pulling some money from her pocket.

Robin sniffed the sandwich Griff had given her. It smelled funny. Deer meat? She tossed the sandwich into the nearest bin and searched her pockets for spare change. Finding some coins, she ordered fries too. When their orders came, she followed Zo-Zo to the condiments table and loaded the fries with ketchup. She lifted her plate and turned.

Brittany loomed in front of her. She seemed so much bigger up close. Robin stared into her thick neck and tried to step around her. But Brittany moved as she moved. Their arms jostled each other, and Robin lost her balance. Her plate of fries skated across the tray, spilled down her front, then clattered to the concrete floor. The cafeteria hushed and dozens of eyes stared at her chest. She gazed down at herself. Drools of ketchup were splattered across her favourite top.

Humiliation flooded through her. As she looked up from her shirt, she heard a soft click and saw Zo-Zo holding her camera. That night, a photo of Robin and her ketchup-stained clothes was posted on the Internet for all the school to see.

# CHAPTER
# SEVEN

Robin sat with Griff on the straw floor of the barn. The puppies had their eyes open now and were crawling all over each other, stepping on each other's backs and heads and anything else that was in the way.

"You'd think someone gave them beer for breakfast," Griff said, chuckling at the drunken way the puppies lost their balance and continually fell over.

Robin laughed. Here in the barn with the puppies was where she was happiest. She loved watching them wiggle and wag their way around, yipping at each other's tails, ears, and noses and biting anything they could get into their mouths. At the moment, one of them was biting Griff's finger.

"Yikes," Griff said, pulling her hand away. "They're getting teeth!"

Robin laughed. "I know!"

It was good to sit down. She and Griff and Squirm had spent the morning moving Relentless and the puppies from Griff's to the barn so they could have more room. Ari was supposed to help, too, but so far she hadn't shown up. Neither had her father. But then he had work as an excuse.

"You sure the puppies will be warm enough out here?" Robin rubbed a puppy's stomach. The skin there was as soft as velvet.

"We'll put the heater on at night," Griff said. "If we need it. Last night it was so warm, it rained instead of snowed. Did you hear it?"

Robin nodded. She remembered waking up to the sound of it drumming on the tin roof of the shed. She looked around the barn. Something inside her still felt uneasy about the puppies being out here. "What if wolves get in?"

"We'll keep the barn door latched. Besides," Griff said, pointing up at the rafters, "don't forget, we've got the protection of our killer owl up there."

Robin tilted her head back and looked at Owlie. She didn't understand how a stuffed bird could keep an eye on anything, but she didn't say that. Besides, she had to admit, she kind of liked the idea of Owlie keeping watch.

Relentless nudged her sleek head against Robin's shoulder.

"I know, you'll take care of them too," Robin said, running her palm along her dog's back. She did this over and over until Relentless shivered with pleasure.

"Where's your sister?" Griff asked. "Wasn't she supposed to help?"

Robin shrugged. "On the phone. With one of her five million new friends."

Griff nodded pensively. "I never made friends easily. Always took me awhile. She got a boyfriend yet?"

"Nope. But there's tons interested — so she says!" Robin sighed. "I guess all that make-up is paying off."

Griff raised an eyebrow but did not speak.

"No!" Griff pulled a puppy they'd nicknamed Tugger away from her bootlaces.

They'd given some of the puppies names. Tugger because he was always pulling on things, Snooze because he fell asleep so easily, and Greedy Guts because she bullied others at the food tray.

"I'm going to get some more clean straw," Griff said. "Be right back."

Robin watched as Tugger yanked Snooze's tail. "Hey!" she said, prodding him away, but he simply turned his attentions to the frayed bottoms of her jeans. She picked him up and tapped his nose with her finger. "Stop being such a troublemaker. I have enough of those in my life as it is."

Of course, she was thinking about Brittany. The incident in the cafeteria had been a while ago now, but, like a broken DVD, it kept replaying on the screen of her mind. Had Brittany meant to flip her lunch tray like that? Robin was convinced she had. She just wished she'd smacked Brittany, right there on the spot. Or at least told her off. But had she? Oh no! She'd just stood there and done nothing. Like some pathetic wuss.

Since then, she'd washed her green shirt five times but hadn't been able to get out the ketchup stains. She couldn't get the sound of the kids laughing out of her mind either. Or stop that stupid photo Zo-Zo had taken from flashing in her memory. Despite her every attempt to leave the event behind, the humiliating images kept chasing after her and swarming her like a gang of thugs.

She had another worry too: Brodie. She kept imagining conversations with him, even fantasies about him walking her home, and the two of them doing homework together. Which was stupid. Beyond stupid. A good-looking guy like Brodie would never be interested in someone like her. Boys wanted real girls. Girls who actually *had* fingernails. And long, silky hair like her sister. But spending time with Brodie would be dangerous. Brittany had made it punch-in-the-face clear that Brodie was *her* property, property she intended to protect violently if necessary.

So, every day, Robin resolved before going to school that she wouldn't look at Brodie, and every day she broke that resolve a dozen times. At least. Besides, she couldn't *not* look at him now that they were paired in this environmental project. It wasn't her fault if life was throwing them together. There was a weird feeling of inevitability about it all. That's how it had felt with her mother too.

When Robin had first found out that her mother was sick, she and everyone in her family had done everything they could to help her get better. Her father had taken over the cooking so her mom could rest, and Robin, Ari, and Squirm had made their own lunches and cleaned their rooms. They had even stopped fighting, at least in front of her.

Their mother had gone on a special diet, taken vitamins, gotten massages and did what she called "visualizations," where she pictured herself being healthy. She lost weight anyway, then she lost her hair, and, finally, she lost her ability to move. At the end, she couldn't even speak.

Throughout it all, Robin had prayed until she got bruises on her knees. One day, despite all her pleading, the worst thing Robin ever could have imagined had happened. "What will be, will be," Aunt Lizzie had said, uncurling Robin's fingers from her mother's hand.

Robin wished she could spit those words right out of her body.

"Hey!" Squirm climbed into the pen. He dropped some old blankets on the floor over the straw. "This will keep them warm," he said. He sat down beside Robin and picked up the smallest puppy. "I'm calling this guy Einstein. He's way smarter than the others." He snuggled the puppy into his neck.

Ari appeared behind him.

"Now you show up," Robin said. "We're all done."

"It's not my fault that you guys did it so fast." Ari extended one of her long slender fingers and rubbed a puppy's ear.

When Griff returned, Squirm said to her, "Did you see that guy in the ATV out in the field?"

"Probably Mr. Big Shot on one of his toys."

They all went to the barn door, where they stood watching an ATV crossing the field. After the previous night's rain, the ground was now covered in slushy snow and the ATV was leaving big muddy tracks in its wake.

"That man's not tall enough to be Rick Kingshot," Griff said, tracking the ATV with her eyes. She crossed her arms. "Must be Conner, his sixteen-year-old. The one who thinks he's a big time hunter. Like his dad."

Ari stepped forward. "That's Conner?" She sounded breathless. "He's like the hottest guy in school."

Griff gave a loud sigh.

Squirm scrunched up his face as he watched the ATV. "What's he doing?"

"That's what I'm trying to figure out," Griff said. "Usually, Conner's going like a bat out of hell." But the ATV was moving slowly, as if in search of something.

Robin saw it first. Something round and black was running ahead of the ATV. A raccoon? But raccoons didn't get that big, did they? She stared harder. When she realized what it was, she tried to say the word, but it caught in her throat. Squirm said it for her. Except he said it with excitement. She would have said it with fear.

"Bear!" Squirm shouted. "It's a bear!"

She reached out and grabbed the back of his jacket, but he wrenched himself free and was off. She lurched after him, caught his arm, and dragged him to a halt.

Squirm yanked his arm away furiously. His face was flushed. "I've never seen a bear, not a real one." He raced across the muddy field. "It's so little … it must be just a baby —"

A baby? An alarm bell went off in Robin's body. If there was a baby bear, there would be a mother nearby. Even she'd heard how vicious mother bears were when it came to protecting their young.

A gun fired. Robin almost jumped out of her boots.

"He's trying to kill it!" Squirm broke into a run.

Robin sped after him, slipping in the mud. The slushy snow soaked the legs of her jeans, but she kept running anyway, jerking her head around every few moments to make sure the mother bear wasn't coming from behind to attack them.

The baby bear was running fast now. Robin was trying to keep her eye on it as she ran, when suddenly it dropped out of sight. What? She stood still, her eyes riveted on the spot where she'd last seen it. How could the bear just disappear? Had the boy shot it? She hadn't heard the gun go off again. She ran forward, not stopping until she reached Squirm. He was looking down into a pile of rocks. She stepped forward to see better. In the middle of the rocks was a deep cylindrical hole.

Robin leaned over and peered into what she realized must be an old well. It smelled of stale water, but there was another smell too. The smell of something wild.

Squirm leaned as far as he could into the hole. Robin, afraid he might fall in, gripped his jeans tightly.

"He's in there all right," Squirm said, pulling himself back. "Way at the bottom. Look at him! Isn't he cool? We've got to help him out."

The ATV pulled up, and Robin straightened.

Conner set his gun into a rack at the side of the ATV and got off. Standing, he looked huge. He was big-boned like his sister, Brittany, and had the same thick blondish hair.

Ari and Griff were approaching, and hearing them, Conner turned. Robin watched as Conner's eyes travelled the length of Ari's body. One side of his mouth rose in a smile.

"Hey," he said. "Haven't I seen you around school?"

Ari's tongue poked out and wet her lips. She smiled.

"What's your name?"

"Ari." Her eyes were bright.

Conner drew himself up taller. He strode over to the well.

Robin watched him carefully. She could see why Zo-Zo had said all the high school girls thought he was good-looking. Not only was he muscular, with big, wide shoulders, but he had a soft, almost angelic-looking face. Despite that, however, there was something about his eyes that didn't look innocent at all.

"That'll be an easy shot with my crossbow," he said glancing down the well.

Squirm paled. "You're going to kill it?"

"No choice. He hasn't got a hope of getting out."

"We'll go down and get him," Squirm said.

Conner laughed. "And get the skin clawed right off of you?" He glanced at Ari as he grabbed a large metal bow from the side of his ATV. "If I put a rope on this crossbow, I'll be able to pull his body out after I shoot him." He turned his attention to the woods across the field. "His mom will be watching. If I can skunk her out of hiding, I'll get myself two bear rugs instead of one." He turned to Ari with warm confidence. "I'll give you one if you like."

Griff stepped forward. "Put that thing away! There's going to be no killing here."

"No?" Conner readied the crossbow.

Griff pushed it aside. "I think you best get back on to your own property. Now! Robin? Squirm? Go get the ladder."

Conner shook his head. "You city people! You don't know squat about nature. That bear has claws like razor blades! They'll shred you to ribbons."

Griff straightened her shoulders and looked at Robin. "The ladder's inside the barn. To the right of the door. The two of you should be able to manage it."

Conner turned to Ari. "Is she crazy?" He put the bow back into its stirrup and patted the seat. "Come on, Ari. I'll take you for a ride."

Griff's eyebrows arched as high as an alarmed cat's back.

Ari tossed her hair over her shoulders and climbed into the passenger seat.

Griff's hand gripped her jaw. "Don't be long."

If Conner heard, he made no sign. He gunned the ATV and charged off, leaving a cloud of blue smoke in its wake.

Squirm waved the smoke away and set off across the field with Robin. He scrunched up his nose. "Wow, those ATVs sure can fart."

# CHAPTER EIGHT

Robin and Squirm trudged through the snowy ruts. It wasn't far to the barn, but Robin kept staring into the trees. A clump of black caught her eye.

"It's the bear! The mother bear! Look!"

Her breath stopped and she stood still, waiting for it to charge from the woods.

"Where?" Squirm challenged. "I don't see anything."

When the clump didn't move, Robin exhaled and started walking again. She slipped but kept staring behind her. Every patch of black seemed to have eyes and fur. What would she do if it attacked? Run? She'd heard somewhere that you were supposed to lie down and play dead if a bear attacked. She couldn't imagine doing that. She'd be too afraid. But she'd probably be too afraid to run, so she'd be doomed.

When they finally reached the barn, she hefted one end of the old wooden ladder and Squirm took the other, and they started back across the field. They hadn't gone far when their dad called to them from the porch of the farmhouse.

"What's going on?"

"A bear, Dad, a bear!" Squirm shouted. "Conner, the boy next door, he was chasing it, then it fell down the well."

Robin watched her dad disappear into the house. She scowled. Didn't he care? Then he reappeared with his medical bag.

"You sure?" he asked, catching up with them. "It should still be hibernating."

"It's tiny," Squirm said.

"It must be."

When they got to the well where Griff was waiting, their dad peered down it for several moments, frowning. Robin could hear the bear whimpering.

"It's only a few weeks old, for Pete's sake!" He looked up and stared into the woods. Creases formed on his forehead. "The mother won't be far."

"Conner wanted to kill it. And the mom!" Squirm's face was full of anguish. "Can we save him, Dad? Can we?"

"Maybe, now that we have a ladder. I'll go down and pull him up. He can't be more than ten pounds —"

"But what about his claws?" Robin asked. She'd picked up a stray cat once, and it had ripped long red scratch lines down her bare arm. From what Conner had said, the bear's claws would be a thousand times more dangerous.

Their father pulled a balaclava and what looked like oven mitts from his bag. "Vets know all about claws…."

Robin grinned. "Smart, very smart."

He pulled on the balaclava. "If you think the baby's claws are scary, think about the mother's! They'll be longer than your fingers. And sharp enough to tear your face off in a single swipe."

"Whoa!" Squirm said. "I'm glad it's you going down there and not me!"

"Once I get him, he's going right back to the wild," their dad said, shoving his hands into the thick mitts. "We're not taking in any baby bears." He squinted into the fields. "We don't want to get his mother's nose out of joint. Mother bears can get nasty. Very nasty."

Robin cringed but helped the others lift the ladder into the well.

She watched her father descend. The further he went, the harder it was to see him, but as she strained over the stone lip of the well, she watched him scoop up the cub. He cradled it under one arm and climbed back up, then sat on the side of the well. The others gathered around.

Now that Robin was up close to it, the bear didn't seem so scary. It was so little. No bigger than a small dog, but it had black, shiny fur, a tan snout, and a crest on its throat.

"He's adorable," she whispered.

"Believe me," her father said. "This guy's no teddy bear." He lifted the bear's paw and showed her its claws.

Griff pressed the tip of a finger against the end of one. "Sharp! No wonder they can climb trees. I could too, if I had spikes like that on the ends of my hands."

"How come he's holding his arm like that?" Squirm asked.

Robin stared, too. There was something odd about one of the bear's front legs.

Her father blew air out his mouth as he stood up. "Let's get it back to the barn where I can examine it properly. Without worrying about 'mom.'"

He handed his medical bag to Robin, and, still cradling the bear, began walking back to the barn. Squirm and Griff picked up the ladder and Robin lugged the medical bag. It was heavy, but Robin always liked carrying it. It was like carrying hope.

She scanned the woods as she went. Now that they had the baby, wasn't the mother even more likely to attack? She yelled out to the others. "What if the mother bear sees us? What if she comes after us?"

"And what if the sky falls in?" Griff called back.

Robin's worry pushed more questions out her mouth. "What should we do? Run?"

Griff waited for her to catch up. "A bear can run way faster than you."

Robin felt a rising sense of panic.

Griff put her free hand on Robin's shoulder. "Settle down, girl. Remember, if she comes, she's coming for her baby. We'll just give her what she wants."

Robin nodded, relieved.

When they got to the barn, the puppies yipped at the gate of their enclosure, and Relentless barked ferociously at the bear cub.

"She knows a wild thing when she smells it," Griff said.

They took the bear into one of the stalls, and their father opened his medical bag. He brought out a stethoscope and placed the end that looked like a big silver medallion on the bear's chest. The bear pawed at the tube.

Robin waited for a few moments then said, "Can I listen?"

"Sure." Her father arranged the stethoscope in her ears.

Robin held her breath, thinking she'd have to be very quiet, but the thubbing sound coming through the stethoscope was strong and rhythmic.

"Wow!" she whispered. *How magical was that!*

Squirm nudged her arm. "Can I listen?"

Robin sighed and gave Squirm the stethoscope. Sometimes having to share things with her brother was a drag.

"Cool," Squirm said, then moved the round end of the stethoscope further down the bear's body. "I hear squishing."

"He's digesting," their father said. "Probably that kid he ate for breakfast."

Squirm's eyes twinkled at his father's joke. "What *do* bears eat anyways?"

"They're omnivores," his father said. "So, pretty much anything — fish, berries, meat —"

"Garbage, if people don't put it away properly," Griff said.

Their father probed the bear's front leg, from his shoulder to his paw. The cub made a yipping sound.

"He's hurt!" Robin said, making a face.

He grimaced. "You got that right. It's broken."

"Can you fix it?" Robin asked.

"I can put a cast on it, but if I did that, I'd have to sedate him. We'd also have to keep him for a few weeks."

"We could keep him here!" Squirm said.

Robin gripped her father's arm. "We'll take care of him." She pressed his arm. "Please?"

Her father shook his head. "We have enough to handle with the puppies. You kids are probably falling asleep at your desks as it is!"

Robin fired back, "I haven't fallen asleep at school once." She didn't mention that she almost had. Several times.

"Me neither," Squirm said.

Griff looked at her son. "It's not much extra time...."

"Don't you get on the bandwagon too," he said. He pushed his fingers through his short brown hair. "You have to have a special permit to keep a wild animal, even for a few days. It wouldn't be legal."

"Legal, shmeegal," Griff said. "No one needs to know."

Squirm looked up at his father. "Please, Dad —"

Robin watched her father roll his lips back into his mouth.

Griff touched his arm. "Remember why you became a vet — to help animals."

He made a huffing sound. "Okay, but you're all sworn to secrecy. I don't want my boss at the clinic finding out. He does everything by the book. Besides, if the authorities get a whiff of what we're doing, we could be fined. They might even euthanize the bear."

Squirm squinted up at his dad. "What's 'euthanize'?"

"Putting to sleep," his father said.

"In other words, killing it," Griff said, bunching her mouth so it looked like a fist.

Robin winced. "They can do that?"

Griff shook her head. "Wild animals don't have rights, Robin. People can kill them at will. For any reason, any time."

Squirm looked astonished. "Can they?"

"Not dogs and cats," his father clarified as he injected a small needle into the bear's front leg. The bear quickly went limp, and he laid the animal gently down in the straw.

"Thanks to the SPCA," Griff added.

Squirm kept his eyes on Griff. "What's the SPCA?"

"Society for the Prevention of Cruelty to Animals," Robin said. She only knew because she was reading a book on the SPCA for a book report. She'd expected the book to be boring but couldn't put it down. The book talked about cats being skinned alive, horses being beaten to death, and a whole bunch of other terrible things that the SPCA had stopped. It was hard to read about but good to read about too.

Her father took some things from his medical bag. "Okay, I'll set his arm and we'll keep him, but only until the bone has healed. Then he's going back to the wild. Is that clear?"

Robin nodded quickly. Squirm did too.

"And *no* more animals. A dog, nine puppies, and a bear is enough."

Robin and Squirm shared a triumphant look and watched as their dad set the bear's broken leg. "Besides, there's not just the authorities we have to worry about, it's the redneck hunters here as well."

Squirm looked at Griff. "What's a 'redneck hunter'? Do they really have red necks?"

Griff laughed. "I think people who were originally called rednecks actually did have red necks because they worked in the fields — their necks got red from the sun."

"A redneck would think it was nuts to set this bear's arm," his father said. "They'd say, 'Let nature take its course.'"

Squirm looked confused. "Are the Kingshots rednecks?"

A smile played on Griff's lips. "Bingo."

After the bear's arm was set in a small cast, the four worked at nailing some heavy fencing around the inside of the stall. Every once in a while, the little cub tried to lift its head, but it was too sedated to hold it up for long.

"I think he knows we're here," Robin said.

"I bet he can smell us," Squirm said.

Griff laughed. "He can smell what you ate for breakfast three days ago."

"I wish I could smell like that," Squirm said.

They lapsed into silence. Robin thought about the soft thudding the bear's heart had made.

"Do you think Conner really would have killed it?" she asked Griff.

Griff snorted. "Yes, I do."

"You see that crossbow?" Squirm said. "It was deadly."

Robin looked at Griff. She felt confused. "But you kill things...."

Griff spoke quietly. "Yes, but I do it with respect. And, I eat the meat. Besides, I'd never kill a *baby*!"

Her son added, "I don't think any self-respecting hunter would."

Griff continued. "The way I figure it, a wild animal would rather die out in nature from the quick bullet of my gun than be loaded into a truck and taken to an abattoir."

She stroked the baby bear. "Conner and his dad, Rick, they don't kill to eat. They kill to feel powerful. You should see the inside of their place. There's antlers and animal heads on every wall. Like trophies. I bet they make Kingshot and Conner feel like big shots every time they look at them."

"But he *is* a big shot," Squirm argued. "Look at all the stuff he's got, trucks, cars, ATVs —"

"Big boy toys." Griff let out a long, slow sigh. "Stuff like that might give you a thrill at first, but it doesn't last." She tousled Squirm's hair. "It just goes to show, you can never have enough of what you don't really want." She stood up. "And speaking of mounting heads on a wall, that's what I'm going to do with Conner's if he doesn't bring Ari back soon."

Her son stopped his hammering. "Ari's with Conner? How did that happen?"

Griff shrugged. "He offered to take her for a ride and she went."

"You shouldn't have let her!"

The sound of the ATV approaching stopped their conversation. Squirm yawned. "Is Conner going to be Ari's boyfriend now?"

Griff dropped the hammer she was holding. "What a dastardly thought. But I can see why she likes him. He's got that choirboy cherubic face, yet he's a bit of a rebel. A lot of girls like that. In my generation, we used to swoon over James Dean."

"What's swoon?"

Griff smiled with amusement. "What your sister is doing."

Robin peeked out the barn door and watched her sister saying goodbye to Conner. When Robin had seen her with other boys, she'd always looked bored, as if she was putting up with them, but now, with Conner, her face was flushed and dreamy.

Robin went back inside and helped arrange more straw in the bear's stall.

Squirm yawned again. "I'm hungry. Can we go now?"

Griff nodded. "Of course. I've got to get some baby food ready. This guy's going to be hungry when he wakes up." She looked at the bear fondly. "Won't you, Mukwa."

"'Mukwa'?" Robin asked.

Griff explained. "It's Ojibway for the word *bear*."

"Cool," Squirm said.

After they left, Robin stretched out on the bale of hay and looked at the cub. He was sleeping with his head tucked into the soft fur of his chest. As if feeling her gaze, he opened his eyes. Becoming agitated, he tried to pull himself up.

Robin spoke to him quietly. "I know. You're wondering where your mom is. But I promise, you will see her again. As soon as your arm's better." The bear seemed to settle at the sound of her voice. "Meanwhile, we're going to take care of you. So, you don't have to be afraid. You and your mom will be back together soon."

Robin wiped her eyes. What was she crying for now?

The baby bear became quiet and closed its eyes. In another few moments, she heard the low rhythmic snuffle of his breathing and knew he was asleep. She smiled. They'd saved the bear from being shot. That was good.

She stood up and checked on Relentless and the puppies. They were all piled on top of one another, legs and tails and snouts going in every direction, but fast asleep. That felt good too.

Whistling, she left the barn.

# CHAPTER NINE

Robin's alarm went off at six. With the bear to feed as well as the puppies, she had to get up even earlier these days. She pulled a jacket over her pajamas and stumbled bleary-eyed towards the barn. As soon as she stepped outside, the brightness of the day greeted her. The sun was out, and it felt warm against her face. No wonder all the snow was melting. There was hardly any in the yard now. She took in a deep breath. The air smelled fresh and new, and it made her feel hopeful and alive.

As usual, Mukwa smelled her coming and was standing at the front of his enclosure when she came in. The creak of the barn door ignited the puppies into a frenzy of ecstatic yips and yelps. Their exuberance at the sight of her made all her tiredness disappear.

She went to the back of the barn and made up Mukwa's formula, then pulled on the oven mitts and tattered old coat that hung beside his enclosure and went in. Mukwa hopped into her lap the moment she sat down. Because of his cast, it was difficult for him to hold the bottle, so she helped him get it into his mouth and held it in place. He made happy little grunting noises as he sucked, and his claws clicked on the plastic sides of the bottle. Feeling his heat through the coat, she relaxed, and a lovely contented feeling moved through her body.

When he was finished with the bottle, he crawled down from her lap and scampered around the enclosure, chasing a ball. It wouldn't roll any more, because he'd inadvertently punctured it, but he swatted it with his cast and chased it around.

"I'll bring you a new one tomorrow," she promised and went to feed the dogs.

The puppies were getting some solid food now, and as soon as she set the bowls on the floor, Greedy Guts tried to eat both her own food and the food of the puppy next to her. Robin picked her up and set her bowl away from the others. When they were all done eating, she took them outside in batches. Relentless trotted beside her, corralling any puppies that strayed.

After the animals were fed, she quickly changed and ran to the bus. Squirm and Ari were already there. Ari's bus came first. When Ari got on, Robin heard some kids call out her name. Then she saw Conner waving her over to sit beside him.

Her own bus was right behind. She got on and sat with Squirm. One or two kids said hi to Squirm, but no one made a special point of saying hi to her. They probably all thought she was weird once that photo of her in the ketchup-soaked shirt had been plastered all over the Internet. She sighed and looked out the window. Would she ever make friends? There were only two possibilities:

Brodie and Zo-Zo. Brodie was out of bounds, and even though she often had lunch with Zo-Zo, she didn't feel relaxed with the girl. How could she? Zo-Zo had put that picture of her with ketchup down her front on her blog. What kind of person would do that? No one she could trust.

Her stomach did a flip as she remembered what was going to happen at school. Today was the day she and Zo-Zo and Brodie were meeting about the environmental project. They were supposed to meet last week, but Mr. Lynch had been sick and they'd had a substitute teacher. She groaned. Why, why, why had she and her family ever moved here?

It wasn't until after recess that Mr. Lynch instructed them to get into their small groups. Robin positioned her chair as far away from the other two as she could.

Zo-Zo tapped her pen on the desk. "Okay, so we've got to come up with a game to make the school greener."

Brodie nodded.

Zo-Zo turned to Robin. "You're the Green Girl — got any ideas?"

Robin tilted her chair back, crossed her arms, and said nothing.

Zo-Zo dug the end of her pen into her palm and stared at Robin. "You're mad, aren't you? About me putting that picture on my blog?"

Robin mashed her lips together. She was going to keep her mouth shut.

Brodie looked at Robin. She felt her stomach drop, just the way it did when she was on the roller coaster at the fair. They both blushed and looked away.

Brodie cleared his throat. "If someone posted a picture of me with ketchup all over my shirt, I wouldn't like it either."

Zo-Zo shot forward in her chair. "I — I just wanted people to see how *mean* Brittany can be. The brat — I didn't mean to make you feel bad, I ..."

Mr. Lynch walked by their table. "Stay on track," he warned.

Brodie nodded. "Yes, sir."

Zo-Zo's eyes didn't move from Robin. "Please don't be mad. You're my hero! You're famous! My dad and I looked you up in the news archives! Your picture was in the paper and everything." She turned to Brodie. "She got this big award."

Robin willed herself not to blush, but she could feel heat rising on her face.

"Cool," Brodie said. "So it is true."

"Did Big Brat Brittany say it wasn't?" Zo-Zo rammed her goggle-like glasses back up her nose.

Robin blushed with anger.

Brodie shrugged. "She didn't say it wasn't true. She just said she wouldn't be surprised if it wasn't. How was she to know?"

"She could have checked it out, like I did," Zo-Zo said, staring him down.

Mr. Lynch walked over to their group again and stood listening.

Brodie made his voice sound authoritative. "I was thinking we could do a contest instead of a game." Mr. Lynch walked away, but Brodie carried on talking about how the contest could work. "We could design an eco-contest. Something that would get people motivated to be greener."

Robin watched as Brodie's face lit up. Her mother's face used to do that. The memory squeezed at her chest. She bit her thumbnail.

Zo-Zo grabbed her pen. "The contest could give points for things like hanging out laundry and turning off the water when you're brushing your teeth. The person with the most points could win something." She grinned, exposing a mouth full of braces. "My dad would donate some prizes. He's a sucker for green stuff."

Robin put her face in her hands. This was all such a waste of time.

"It would be really cool to actually get people *doing* green things," Brodie said. "Like walking to school —"

"Your girlfriend won't be happy about that one," Zo-Zo said, looking from Brodie to Robin. "Brittany's dad drives a Hummer. My dad says it must come with its own oil well."

Brodie's face darkened. "She's not my girlfriend."

Brodie wasn't Brittany's boyfriend? Robin's stomach did another dip.

Zo-Zo let out a snort of air. "She sure acts like she is."

"I know. I wish she'd stop."

"Five more minutes," Mr. Lynch called.

Zo-Zo began writing down the ideas they'd come up with. "We could have points for when people use a clothesline instead of a dryer."

"Yeah," said Brodie. "That's good."

Zo-Zo turned to Robin. "You make a suggestion. You're the expert."

Robin sat on her hands. "What good is getting a few people to hang out laundry going to do?" She shook her head. It was like splashing drops of water on a bonfire.

Brodie's brow furrowed. "So we should do nothing?"

Robin looked into his earth brown eyes. "There's no point. It's too late — things have gone too far."

A muscle in Brodie's jaw twitched. "You can't know that. No one can."

Robin sighed. Once upon a time she'd believed there was hope, too. Once upon a time she'd thought that if everyone took action, the planet might survive. She didn't believe that any more.

Brodie sat forward. "Look, even if the odds *are* bad, we still have to try. We can't just stand by and let bad things happen. I can't, anyway."

Robin shrugged and said nothing.

Brodie was talking to Zo-Zo now. "I just think we have to do everything we can."

Zo-Zo shrugged. "Listen, you guys, whether we can save the planet or not, we still have a project to do!"

Robin yawned and gave a small nod. She wasn't going to risk failing the assignment just because she thought it was a waste of time. Feeling a sneeze coming, she reached into her pocket for a tissue. When she pulled it out, some dog biscuits came too.

Zo-Zo beamed at her. "Oh yeah, you've got puppies, don't you?"

"Puppies?" Brodie asked.

"Didn't you hear? Robin crawled on the ice and saved a dog. A dog that then had a bunch of puppies, right? That's what my brother said your brother told him and —"

Robin was going to strangle Squirm the moment she got home.

Brodie eyed her with interest. "Wow. You rescued a dog?"

"Can I see the puppies?" Zo-Zo pleaded. "I'll take some pictures, and we can put them up on the Internet instead of that one of you wearing ketchup."

"Sure," Robin said. Anything to get rid of the ketchup photo.

The bell rang for recess. Robin grabbed an apple and followed Zo-Zo down the hall.

"He likes you," Zo-Zo said.

Robin shrugged. "I don't think so."

"His eyes get all soft when he looks at you," Zo-Zo said.

Robin tossed her apple into the air nervously. If he wasn't Brittany's boyfriend, that was okay, wasn't it? At the end of the hall, she pushed through the big, metal doors that led to the schoolyard. Brittany and a gang of kids clogged the area just outside the door. As Robin tried to get past them, she dropped her apple.

"Oh, the poor little klutzy-klutz," Brittany said.

She spread her arms wide and eased the kids back away from the apple. Then she lifted her leg and stomped down hard, squashing it. "There's your apple, Green Queen."

The other kids craned forward. Some laughed and pointed at the apple pulp.

Robin looked at Brodie. He was standing at the far rim of the gang. Their eyes met, then he looked away.

Robin remembered the words he'd said in class just a few moments ago. *"You can't just let bad things happen and do nothing."*

If he meant that, why was he letting a bad thing happen right now? To her?

# CHAPTER TEN

Robin awoke to the sound of icy rain pellets ticking against the glass of her window. A few days ago, it had been warm and spring-like, but now, even though it was halfway into April, winter was back. She pulled the pillow over her head and was almost asleep again when she heard a strange scritching noise. What was that?

She turned over and opened her eyes grumpily. Ari was rolling a thick line of masking tape down the wall. When she reached the floor, she rolled it along the rug and up the other wall. Now that she had a clear demarcation between her side of the room and Robin's side, she made pincers with her fingers, picked up a folder and tossed it into Robin's area. The notebook splayed open, papers flying out.

"Hey! Don't! That's my book report."

Ari's face was cold and resolute. "Then don't put it on *my* side of the room. From now on, I don't want you to even *step* on my side of the room."

"That's stupid," Robin said. It was also impossible. "You just don't want me reading all that love stuff you write about Conner."

Her guess had been right on, for Ari's hand dove under her pillow. She pulled her diary out, checked to see that the lock was still intact, then dropped it into her purse. "You're just jealous."

Their father appeared in the doorway. "Okay, you two. Enough." He looked at Ari. "Don't forget, I'm driving you to the dentist this morning. I'm going to grab a quick shower, so get yourself some breakfast, then we'll go."

Her father looked at Ari fondly, and Robin turned away. Why didn't he ever look at her that way? Was it her fault if Ari looked so much like their mother?

Ari glared at her dad. "Mom would have made her clean it up." She whisked past him.

Robin saw her father's eyes moisten. Was he going to cry? She felt a heat rise in her chest.

"Can't you at least unpack your boxes?" he said.

Any warmth Robin felt for him disappeared. She didn't want to unpack boxes. That would mean she was agreeing to be here, and she wasn't. She turned her face to the wall.

Her father spoke, his voice gentle. "It will get easier."
She didn't move. *Yeah right.*

When Robin heard him go downstairs, she turned and stared out the window. Freezing rain. That meant the roads would be slippery. What if her father and Ari got in an accident? A sick feeling settled in her stomach. She hated it when she had thoughts like this but had no idea how to stop them.

She pulled herself up and got dressed. It was Squirm's turn to feed the animals, so she could take her time. She picked her book report up from the floor, smoothed the pages and went downstairs. Ignoring Ari, she was going to put the book report right into her backpack, but placed it in front of Griff instead. Her grandmother picked it up and began reading.

Robin poured herself some cereal and ate it while Griff turned the pages. The report looked tiny in her big hands.

Squirm came in from the barn and picked up an apple.

"Wash your hands first," Ari ordered.

Squirm rolled his eyes and looked at Robin.

Robin stared at her sister. Every time either of them came back from the barn, Ari acted like they were covered in toxic waste.

Griff closed the report and shook her head. "Shocking the way animals used to get treated."

"The parts about animals getting beaten or starved, I could hardly read them," Robin said.

"Cruelty to animals is disgusting," Ari said. She straightened her back and set her chin in that way she always did when she made a declaration.

Squirm grimaced. "Then how come you were going to let your *boyfriend* shoot the baby bear?"

Robin expected her sister to retort, "He's *not* my boyfriend," as she always did, but Ari said nothing.

A wistful look crossed Griff's face. "Love is blind."

Their dad came into the kitchen. Ari gathered her things and they left.

Griff patted the bright red folder. "Well done, my girl."

Robin felt herself relax. She'd been telling herself she didn't care if she did well on the book report, but still....

Griff handed Robin the book report and hugged her hard. Robin pulled away quickly, stuffed the book report into her backpack and followed Squirm out the door. When they were on the bus, Robin put the pack on her lap to keep it safe and looked out the window.

"I'm going to put one of those old tires in Mukwa's cage after school," Squirm said. "Bet he'd love that."

"Shh!" Robin hissed. He'd already blabbed to half the school about Relentless and the puppies. She didn't want him doing the same about the bear.

The bus pulled into the school parking lot. Before getting off, Robin checked to see if Brittany was around. When she didn't see the bully, Robin hurried to her classroom. She felt relieved when she got to the safety of her desk.

She glanced over to the far side of the classroom. Brodie was trying to pull his books out of his backpack, and Brittany kept trying to get him to look at something in her notebook. Robin noticed how Brodie's eyebrows knitted with irritation at Brittany's interruptions, but she also saw that he did nothing to stop them. What was it with this boy? She was still mad at him for not saying anything when Brittany had squashed her apple, but then a new thought poked its head into her awareness, like a tiny seedling. Maybe Brodie felt as bullied by Brittany as she did. That thought diluted her anger toward him.

At that very moment, Brittany tossed a dark look her way.

"All right, class, let's come to order," Mr. Lynch said and gave the morning announcements. When he finished, he told the class to split into their small groups. Robin made sure she sat with her back turned towards Brittany.

Zo-Zo read out the final questions for the eco-contest, and when they had all agreed, she said, "We need to give this little eco-project of ours a name. Something cool. I know! How about 'The Extreme Green Eco-Contest'?"

"Not bad," Brodie said. He was drawing pictures of animals in the margins of his notebook.

They tossed out various ideas. Robin finally said, "How about, 'Your Big Fat Footprint'?" She was only half serious.

Brodie jumped on the idea. "That's awesome!"

Zo-Zo frowned at Brodie. "You always like her ideas better."

"No, I don't!" Brodie reddened. "It's just that the footprint thing would make a great logo. Look." He drew a large footprint. "We could colour it green and put it on white T-shirts. If your dad was still willing to donate stuff, we could get a bunch made up and give them away as prizes."

"Yeah, my dad would do that. He already told me he'll donate some prizes. He also said that if we wanted to have our questionnaire printed, to, like, make it look really professional, he'd take it to the place that does the paper."

Brodie gave Zo-Zo a high five. "Now you're talking."

He raised his hand to give a high five to Robin as well.

Robin lifted her hand. When hers touched Brodie's, she felt a zing race from her fingers to her elbow.

Zo-Zo twirled her pen. "Before we get the questionnaire printed, I think we should do it ourselves. Just to see how we score."

"I'm up for that," Brodie said.

They each pulled out a blank piece of paper, and Zo-Zo read out the questions.

Zo-Zo finished scoring hers first. "Bummer. According to our point system, I'm going to need four whole planets to stay alive."

Brodie slapped down his pen. "That's nothing, I'm going to need six!"

Robin shrugged. *I told you*, she wanted to say.

Zo-Zo peeked at Robin's page. "How many planets do you need to stay alive?"

"One and a half."

"Wow —" Brodie said, admiration filling his face.

"It's still pathetic," Robin said.

Zo-Zo grimaced. "Our contest is just going to make people feel hopeless."

"But it *is* hopeless," Robin said.

Mr. Lynch wandered the isles. "Three minutes left."

Zo-Zo looked down. "Maybe our eco-contest isn't such a good idea after all."

Robin rolled her eyes. If they'd listened to her, they wouldn't be in this mess.

Brodie straightened in his seat. "No, it *is* a good idea. We've just run into a snag, that's all."

Zo-Zo chewed her pen. "You call this a snag? It feels more like a brick wall!"

"I know, but we'll figure it out."

Robin said nothing. Although she still thought what they were doing was a waste of time, she admired Brodie for not giving up.

The bell sounded. Later, Robin found Zo-Zo in the cafeteria at lunch. She also found Brodie. He was sitting by himself.

Zo-Zo followed Robin's eyes. "Maybe he's decided to dump the Big Brat after all." She turned her gaze to Robin. "He'll be your boyfriend next, bet you anything."

Robin suppressed a smile. "No way."

"You're hot."

Air snorted out Robin's nose. She covered her face with her hand, embarrassed. "Me? Hot? I don't think so."

"At least you don't wear glasses. And your body's not the size of a seven-year-old." Zo-Zo pushed her glasses back up her nose.

Robin was trying to figure out what to say when Zo-Zo let out a laboured breath. "My dad says that pretty girls do better in the first half of life. Smart ones do better later. I just have to wait, that's all."

Brittany walked by with her tray of food. Robin and Zo-Zo watched as she went over to where Brodie was sitting, pushed away a kid who was about to sit beside him, and sat down.

"So much for my break-up theory," Zo-Zo said. "But I don't get it. If she's not his girlfriend, why does he let her act like she is?"

"Maybe he's scared of her. Like I am," Robin said.

Zo-Zo said. "I think half the school's scared of her."

After lunch, the whole class went to an assembly in the auditorium. When they came back, Mr. Lynch asked everyone to hand in their book reports. Robin leaned over to get her backpack.

She jerked from one side of her desk to the other, looked underneath her desk, then behind her desk. Twisting her whole body so she could peer under the desks nearby, she couldn't see her backpack anywhere. Panic rose from her belly to her throat. She tried to swallow it down.

"My pack …" She nudged Zo-Zo hard. "Did you see it?"

Zo-Zo quickly put her own report on the teacher's desk and helped Robin look.

"Is there anyone who *isn't* handing in their report?" Mr. Lynch asked.

Robin cringed and lifted her hand. Mr. Lynch's face darkened with disapproval. Robin lowered her eyes. Her face burned.

"Ten marks off for every day it's late," he told her.

"But I did it," Robin cried. "I brought it, but someone took it, someone —"

Mr. Lynch shook his head as if he'd heard excuses like this a thousand times.

Robin bit the side of her thumb. She would *not* cry!

An hour later, Robin and Zo-Zo were walking down the hall to gym class when Robin remembered that her backpack not only contained her book report but her gym stuff too.

"Now I'm going to get a detention for not having my gym clothes."

Zo-Zo bunched her mouth into a tight ball. Then words burst out of her. "Your backpack's got to be somewhere. Whoever took it had to stash it somewhere!" An idea flashed across her face. "The girls' washroom!"

They raced down the hall and stormed into the washroom. Sure enough, the pack was there, stuffed into the garbage bin. They pulled it out and found Robin's rumpled gym stuff inside, but no book report.

Robin's eyes stung. She hated this school.

# CHAPTER
# ELEVEN

Robin trudged up the muddy lane to the farmhouse, not caring how dirty her boots got. Inside she kicked them off, grabbed some cookies, and headed into her dad's office. She would print the book report now and be done with it. The room was empty, but the printer was whirring away. Robin lifted one of the freshly printed pages from the tray. It was a richly coloured page from a clothing catalogue. Robin checked to see how many pages were still to print. Twenty! But there weren't twenty pages of paper left in the paper tray. There were only three. She needed those three for her report. She hit the "stop" button.

Ari swept into the room. "I'm not finished." She punched "start" and the printer whirred into action.

Robin jabbed the "stop" button. "I need this paper. I have to print my book report. For *school*!" She hoped the word *school* would add the weight she needed.

"But I need a dress. For the *dance*! There's one in this catalogue that —" Ari pushed the "start" button again.

Robin pulled the power cord from the wall. There was no way she was going to let Ari's need to impress Conner override her school work.

"Plug it back in!" Ari ordered. "And get your own paper!"

Robin pulled the other end of the power cord, and tucking it under her arm, ran from the room. She didn't know who she hated more, Brittany or her sister.

Stuffing the cord into her coat pocket, she pushed her feet into her muddy boots and took off for the barn. There she found Griff sitting in front of Mukwa's cage.

"Oh my, who peed on your cornflakes?" Griff asked, regarding her with concern. She patted the bale of hay beside her. "Come on, talk to me. What's up?"

Robin slumped down, shoved her chin into her hands and said nothing. Relentless whined and licked her knuckles.

"Get your book report in?"

"Someone stole it." Robin sat up, yanked a strand of hay from the bale and began tearing it to bits. "I have to print it out again, but Ari's using all the paper."

"Someone took your report? Was it the girl who dumped your lunch tray?"

Robin stared at her grandmother. How did Griff know about that? "She thinks I like her boyfriend, Brodie. Except he isn't her boyfriend. She just wants him to be."

Griff gently tucked some hair behind Robin's ear so she could see her face. "*Do* you like him?"

Robin hid her face in her hands, but Relentless nudged her until she looked up. She began stroking the dog's back.

Griff's voice was soft. "I thought so." She breathed in deeply and let the air out slowly. "You like who you like. That's just the way things are. Is this Brodie Gentles you're talking about?"

Robin nodded.

"I can see why you'd like him. I used to know his dad. His dad's a fine man. Or was —"

"What do you mean, 'was'?"

"Don't know if I should be telling you this, but you'll probably find out anyways. Can't keep anything a secret in a small town. His dad's been hitting the bottle pretty hard over the last few years."

"Does he, like, get drunk?"

"From what I hear. Not that people always say the truth." Griff frowned.

Robin tried to think about what it would be like to have a dad who had a drinking problem. She'd hate that.

"So the girl you're talking about must be Brittany, Rick Kingshot's daughter. And Conner's sister. My goodness, life gets complicated."

"Now she's out to get me."

They lapsed into silence. Griff filled the puppy bowls with the dried kibble the puppies were now eating. As usual, Greedy Guts raided the food of the others. Griff picked her up by the scruff of the neck and tossed her to the back of the pack. "Just like there are greedy puppies and smart puppies and puppies who are just big love mutts, it's the same with people. You get all kinds. That's just the way it is."

Robin ground her fist into her palm. "Makes me want to be mean back."

Griff hooted with laughter. "I want to be mean to Rick Kingshot sometimes, too. Especially when he starts harassing me about selling the property. Goodness, I've let the air out of his tires, shouted at him to his face, taken the spark plugs out of his snowmobiles — all in my mind, of course. And I've loved every minute of it." She wiped the wet mirth from her eyes and became serious. "But I don't think it would feel so good if I actually *did* any of those things. I think the fantasies are probably better than the reality."

After a few moments of quiet, she said, "I know it's a bit of a stretch to think this way, but people who do mean things, bossy people, bullies and the like, they're usually unhappy and scared themselves."

Brittany scared? That was hard for Robin to believe.

"Take that girl Brittany. If she were happy and felt good about herself, sure, she might want Brodie, but she wouldn't boss everyone else around her to get him, and she wouldn't be stealing other kids' book reports! That's got to feel crappy doing something like that."

Robin shook her head. She didn't want to think of Brittany in any way that lessened her anger. She threw her hands in the air. "So, what are you saying, that I should just let her do mean things? And what about Ari?" she shrieked. "She's *always* being mean! Am I supposed to just shut up and let her?"

Griff frowned. "Don't be too hard on Ari. She's hurting. Like you are."

"She's got a funny way of showing it," Robin retorted.

"Listen, we're all still dealing with the loss of your mom. And we're all doing that in our own way. What you've got to realize is that each person deals with their loss differently. Some people get hard, others get bitter, some go for control. But people do what they do because they're scared. Losing someone you love is scary. Probably the scariest thing of all."

Robin looked into her grandmother's eyes. They were intense and impassioned.

"Ari will heal. As we all will. And who knows, maybe the two of you will be friends again."

"I don't think so."

"You used to be friends."

"I know, but that was *before*!"

"Yes, but things change. And then they change again." Griff rubbed her large hands on her thighs. "Meanwhile, just try and not give in to the part of you that wants to be mean back." She slapped her legs and stood up. "Come on, let's see what we can do about the printer before your sister uses up the last of the paper."

"She won't use the last of the paper," Robin said.

"No?"

Robin pulled the printer cord from her pocket.

Griff raised her eyebrows. "At least you didn't strangle her with it."

They looked at each other and laughed. As Robin stood up, there was a loud noise outside. Relentless pricked her ears and growled.

"Let's hope that isn't the mother bear," Griff whispered. "I saw her prowling around the field earlier today." She edged towards the barn door, picking up a pitchfork as she went.

The door burst open. Zo-Zo charged in.

Griff's hand flew to her chest. "Heavens, child. You scared the daylights out —"

"Look what I've got!" Zo-Zo hefted a box on top of a hay bale then stopped and stared into the stall where the bear was. "Yikes! Is that what I think it is?"

"Yes, but don't tell anybody," Robin said.

"They wouldn't believe me if I did," she said, turning her attention back to the box she'd brought. From inside came high-pitched mewing. Zo-Zo gently peeled back the flaps.

"Ohhhhhh! Kittens," Robin crooned. She reached in to stroke the little balls of black fur. Then she saw the white stripes and yanked her hand away. "Skunks?"

Griff beamed. "I *love* skunks." She picked one up and cradled it in the palm of her hand, stroking it with the other.

Robin looked at her worriedly. "Won't it spray?"

"Too young for that sort of nonsense," Griff said.

"Dad and I found these on the side of the road," Zo-Zo said. "The mother was killed by a car. There was blood everywhere." She grimaced.

Griff made happy little cooing sounds as she petted the baby. "Oh, you poor little orphans!"

"My dad called the animal shelter," Zo-Zo said, "but they only take domestic animals, like cats and dogs."

Robin touched one of the babies. Its fur was silky soft.

Behind them, Mukwa made some snorfling sounds.

Zo-Zo looked at Robin. "And you have a baby bear in your barn because —?"

Robin explained. "He fell down a well and we saved him. He's got a broken arm, but he's going back to the wild as soon as he's better. No one's supposed to know about him, okay?"

Zo-Zo swallowed. "Got it." She turned back to the skunks. "My dad and I can't keep the skunks. Our house is too small. Since you've got the barn and everything, can you take them?"

Robin's eyes went from Zo-Zo to Griff. "Dad said no more animals."

Zo-Zo nodded. She bit her bottom lip. "Would your dad have to know?"

"If we put them at the back, he probably wouldn't find out." Robin scrutinized her grandmother's face. "Would you tell?"

Griff put the baby back in the box and smiled. "Tell? Tell about what?"

The skunks began mewing again. "They're hungry," Robin said.

Zo-Zo nodded. "Starving."

Griff suppressed a smile. "But let's say there *were* skunks here. Because of what you learned feeding the puppies, you'd know how to feed these little critters as well. With the feeding bottles. The food is different, but if you came to the cabin in a little while, you just might find some food on the counter." She waved and went off.

Robin grinned and waved back.

Zo-Zo stared after her. "That's your granny?" Robin nodded. "You're lucky. Mine knits socks and watches game shows."

# CHAPTER TWELVE

For the next week, Robin and Zo-Zo passed notes all day long at school as they tried to come up with names for the skunks. It should have been easy to name them, because each of them looked so different. That had surprised her. She had always thought that all skunks had two white stripes, but that wasn't so. Each of the babies had its own unique markings, some with one fat stripe, others with one fat one and a skinny one, some with no stripes at all.

One day after school, Robin and Zo-Zo were reviewing the names as they waited for Brodie to show up for their eco-contest meeting in the library. Robin wished they weren't even having a meeting. First of all, she didn't see how they were going to solve the problem about the depressing questionnaire. There was nothing that wasn't depressing about the environment. Secondly, she was still upset about Brodie saying nothing when Brittany had squashed her apple.

Robin reviewed all the names for the skunks and underlined the ones she liked best. Meanwhile, Zo-Zo searched through the library shelves and came back with a book. "Look, it's all about skunks." They sat close and opened it up.

"Can we tell Brodie about the skunks?" Zo-Zo asked, flipping the pages.

"I don't think we should tell *anyone*. If my dad finds out, I'll be grounded for life."

Zo-Zo sat back and crossed her arms. "Oh, come on — Brodie wouldn't tell. Not if we made him promise. He's cool."

"Me, cool? Glad you noticed," Brodie said, breezing into the library. He plunked his books down on the table. "I figured it out."

Zo-Zo looked up at him. "Figured what out?"

"How to make our contest less depressing. All we have to do is get people to do exactly what I did. Fill out the questionnaire twice."

Zo-Zo and Robin both stared at him.

"Remember how pathetic my score was the first time I did it? I felt really down about it, so, when I went home, I changed some things, then I did it again and my score was *way* better. That made me feel really good."

Robin wanted to stay mad at him but found it too hard to. "What kind of things did you do?"

"Nothing huge. I, like, changed our light bulbs to those weird-looking environmental ones, then I put up a clothes line, and got my dad to install one of those water-saving shower heads. Oh, yeah, and I got my mom to make veggie burgers. When I did the questionnaire again, my score went way up." He grinned at them. "That's the way we should do it with everybody."

"Oh, I get it," Zo-Zo said, tapping her pen excitedly. "The first time is kind of like an assessment or something. It just shows people where they're at in terms of being green. But then we give people a chance to do better. That's cool. Really cool."

"And the person who makes the most changes wins!" Brodie said.

"Yeah!" Zo-Zo's pen tapping quickened. "After people do the questionnaire once, we could give them a list of things they could do if they wanted a higher score." She grinned. "Then we'd really ace the project."

"Yeah!" Brodie said. He turned and looked at Robin. "This probably all sounds pathetic to you, but the way I figure it, if we can get a whole lot of people doing a whole lot of small things, the total could be huge."

Robin couldn't really argue. She found his excitement infectious. "Maybe we should take the questionnaire to other classes and get more kids involved."

Brodie's smile became huge. "Great idea. We could make this really big."

Zo-Zo ping-ponged from Robin to Brodie. "If we go big like this, my dad will want to do an article on us for the newspaper!"

Brodie preened his hair. "I've always wanted to have my picture in the paper." He grinned at Robin. "Told you guys it would all work out."

Zo-Zo leaned over and pulled a package of papers from her backpack. "Now that we're back on track, take a look at this. It's a mock-up of our questionnaire."

Robin looked at the freshly printed contest sheet. It was printed in a rich green and blue, and the questions had been done in white with little boxes to fill out beside each one. She had to admit it looked great.

Brodie held one up and whistled. "Sweet!"

"Okay, it's a go," Zo-Zo said. "I'll call my dad at lunch. If they print it today, we could have the printed contest sheets by morning. That way we can hand them out tomorrow."

Motivated now, they spent the next fifteen minutes brainstorming ideas for the fact sheet. Within twenty minutes, they'd come up with over twenty things people could do to be greener. Zo-Zo wrote them down and promised to work them up into a fact sheet.

"Okay," Brodie said. "If we hand out the first round of the eco questionnaires tomorrow, we'll have them back by the weekend. Then all we'll have to do is score them."

"Let's do the scoring together," Zo-Zo said. She turned to Robin. "If we meet at your place, Brodie can see the bear and the sk —" Zo-Zo's threw her cupped hand over her mouth.

Robin stared at Zo-Zo in disbelief.

Brodie blinked. "You have a bear?"

Robin glared at Zo-Zo, then turned to Brodie. "Don't tell anyone, okay?"

His face had a shy, dreamy expression. "I have a thing about bears."

Zo-Zo scrutinized him. "What do you mean, 'a thing'?"

"One tried to maul me when I was a baby. My bassinette was outside, and this bear came right up, my mom says to eat me, but I think it was just saying hello.

I *love* bears." He turned to Robin. "Can I come and see it? Please?"

Brodie looked at Robin. "How about Saturday?"

Robin wasn't sure what to do. The safest thing was to say no. However, if Brodie and Zo-Zo came on Saturday, her father would be at the clinic, so they'd be able to play with the animals at their leisure. And her father wouldn't be the wiser. She just might get away with it. But what if she didn't get away with it?

"I work in the morning, but I can come after that," Brodie prodded.

"Okay, Saturday it is," Zo-Zo said.

Robin heard the word "sure" slip out of her mouth.

On the weekend, sunshine blasted through Robin's window, making it easy for her to get out of bed. Wanting to get the animals fed, and fed quickly, she skipped breakfast and headed outside. The day was windy but bright and seemed to rush towards her like a best friend. She smiled. Zo-Zo and Brodie were coming today. How good was that? She stepped quickly towards the barn.

"Guess what?" she told Mukwa as she went into his enclosure and began feeding him. "You're going to meet my friends today!"

Mukwa looked at her as if he totally understood.

"This bear is so smart," she said to Griff when she heard her come into the barn.

"All bears are smart," Griff said. "That's why the Natives hold them in such high esteem. They believe bears are equal, if not superior, to man, with the same intelligence, memory, you name it."

The puppies started to yip and bark for their breakfast. Robin covered her ears.

"Hold your horses," Griff shouted over the din. She put a handful of food into each bowl and stood back as the puppies wolfed it down. She laughed. "Breakfast in fifteen seconds flat. That might be a record." She looked at Robin. "You feeding those other animals we don't have?"

"Oh, the skunks," Robin said, clueing in. She nodded. "As soon as I'm finished with Mukwa."

"I'll take the puppies out then." At the word "out," there was an explosion of yipping and yelping. Griff opened the enclosure, and the pack of puppies bolted towards the barn door and ran outside.

"Come on, Relentless," Griff said. "You better come along and help me keep these babies from running off in ten different directions." Relentless ran ahead, and Griff hurried after them. "I might be getting too old for this."

Robin hurried to feed the skunks. She had hidden them at the back of the barn, and so far not even Squirm knew about them. She didn't want him to know. Normally, she fed them quickly and left so he wouldn't come in and find her with them, but he had slept over at his friend Tom's last night, so this morning she didn't have to worry.

She made up some formula and took it and some needleless syringes into their enclosure. Very gently, she picked up one of the skunks and held it in the palm of her hand. It was no bigger than a small egg. Carefully, she tilted the baby skunk's head back and eased the syringe into its minuscule mouth. As she pressed the plunger, most of the food went in, but some came back out again. This always happened when she went too fast. *Slow down*, she told herself, but it was hard. She felt so revved up. Brodie was going to be here. She was excited and nervous all at the same time.

She eased the next bit of food into the baby skunk more slowly. This time, the whole amount went in, and she could actually see the skunk's belly expanding. She smiled. It felt so good to be able to help them survive. Who knew what would have happened to them if she hadn't taken them in. They probably would have died. She didn't like having to disobey her father, but hopefully he'd never know. She'd feed them until they were strong enough to survive then release them back into the wild. Her father would never find out they had even been there.

She was just about finished feeding when she heard someone come into the barn. She tensed. She knew it wasn't Griff, because she could hear the puppies way off in the field. Her father had already left for the clinic. But what if he'd come back for some reason? Or maybe it was Ari? No, Ari never came out here.

Hurriedly, she tried to gather up the skunks, but they were spread out all over the hay — she didn't have a chance of hiding them now. She heard footsteps coming closer and looked up.

Her brother stepped around the corner. He looked as surprised to see her as she was to see him.

"Squirm! What are you doing here?"

He quickly moved a basket he'd been carrying behind his back. Seeing the skunks, he dropped to his knees. "Wow!" He laughed and began to touch them excitedly.

Robin peeked into the basket Squirm had tried to conceal. She could see something moving beneath the cloth that was covering it. She steeled herself. "Look, we're not supposed to take any more animals —"

"You should talk," Squirm said.

Robin lifted the blanket. Cuddled together at the bottom was a nest of babies. Robin looked at their tiny sleeping bodies. "Squirrels?"

Squirm grinned. "That wind must have knocked their nest down. Tom and I found them this morning."

"I hope you told him to keep his mouth shut."

Squirm tensed. "I'll tell him when he comes over later to see them."

"He's coming? Here? But he'll see the bear and —"

"So? *Your* friends are coming over. We'll just swear everyone to secrecy."

Robin frowned. Keeping the animals secret was turning out to be as hard as keeping ants in a pocket.

The baby squirrels were mewing for food, so Robin arranged a place for them and helped Squirm feed them. After they'd finished, she ran to the house for a shower. She tried on three different outfits and combed her hair several different ways. Finally, she threw the hairbrush into the sink. Enough. She was starting to act like her sister.

A few minutes later, she heard Relentless barking and went outside to wave at Zo-Zo's dad as he pulled away, leaving Zo-Zo standing there with a big pile of papers.

"The eco-contests?" Robin asked.

"Yup. All twenty-five of them," Zo-Zo said. "I can't wait to see how people did."

Brodie rode up just then on a new bike.

Zo-Zo ran a finger along the shiny chrome. "Wow, your dad buy you this?"

Brodie rolled his eyes. "You kidding? My dad only spends money on beer." He rubbed the mirror with his sleeve. "Brittany's dad got it for me."

Zo-Zo threw a glance at Robin. "You got this from Mr. Kingshot?"

Brodie looked away. "I work for him on weekends. He gets me stuff sometimes."

He positioned the bike on its stand and followed them into the barn. "So, where's this bear?"

Zo-Zo whispered to Robin. "Maybe that's why he hangs out with Brittany. To get stuff!"

Robin stood still for a moment, considering this. Would Brodie do something like that? She followed Zo-Zo into the barn.

Brodie stood in front of the bear cub's cage. "Whoa." His tone was hushed. "What happened to his arm?"

Robin explained about the bear's fall into the well.

"Conner Kingshot wanted to kill him!" Zo-Zo said. "Isn't that right, Robin?"

Brodie looked troubled. "My dad hunts. He's got a deer's head in the garage. Freaks me out every time I go out there. This big animal head with glassy eyes, staring at me. My dad even bought me a gun. Wanted me to practice on rabbits in the backyard, but I couldn't do it. I mean, how do you kill something as big and beautiful as a deer?" He shivered. "Or a bear? I'm probably just a gutless chicken, but —"

A warm feeling of sympathy washed into Robin's chest. She handed Brodie a piece of apple. "Here, give him an apple. He loves apples. But put this on first." She handed him the oven mitt.

Brodie edged towards the cage. "Hey there, beautiful bear. Want this apple? Come on, come and take it. You'll like it."

Mukwa reached out and took the apple. Brodie grinned, and before Robin could stop her, Zo-Zo took a picture.

"It's okay," Zo-Zo said, eyeing Robin. "I'll just take a few for the three of us."

Suddenly, Griff arrived back from her long walk with the dogs, and the puppies swarmed them, yipping at their legs, vying for attention. Robin began herding them back into their enclosure. Brodie reached down and grabbed one as it raced by. Relentless barked, nervous about a stranger holding one of her brood. Brodie knelt down and spoke to her quietly until Relentless leaned into him and let him rub her ears. Robin noticed that he did it just the way Relentless liked.

When they had all the puppies rounded up, Griff went back to her cabin, and Robin, Brodie, and Zo-Zo sat on the straw and played with them. Brodie lay back. "I can't believe you have a bear. I even dream about bears." He let the puppies crawl all over him. "But I love dogs, too." He picked one up.

"That's Snooze," Robin told him.

"I wonder if my mom would let me have a puppy," he said.

Zo-Zo snapped a close-up of Snooze. "Show her this and she'll melt. I'm going to ask my dad if I can have one, too."

"I hope you both take one," Robin said. "Then I can still see them."

"Maybe Brittany can have one too," Brodie said. He pointed to Greedy Guts. "Maybe that one."

Robin and Zo-Zo laughed.

"What?"

Robin tried to explain. "That one has some particular characteristics —"

"That would match Brittany's perfectly." Zo-Zo suppressed a grin.

"Know what we could do?" Brodie said. "When you need to find homes for them, we could take them to the market, maybe even pick out people we think would be good dog owners."

Robin noticed the "we" word. It sailed through her like a kite.

"Let's show him the skunks," Zo-Zo said.

"We've got some squirrels, too," Robin said. "They just came in." She led them down to the far end of the barn.

Brodie grinned. "You've got a regular animal shelter here."

Robin winced. "Don't say that. If my dad finds out, I'll get *killed!*"

Brodie nodded solemnly. Zo-Zo took pictures of the skunks, and the three of them were laughing at their antics when Squirm appeared.

"Dad's coming." He sounded breathless. "He just called."

"He's coming here? Now?" Robin felt her shoulders leap to her ears. Why was he coming home?

Squirm read the question on her face. "He's driving Ari somewhere."

Robin looked at her friends. "Let's go up to the house." Hopefully, she'd have everyone working away at the kitchen table by the time her father arrived, and he'd never suspect a thing.

Zo-Zo led the way. "We have to start marking the contest anyway."

At the house, they cleared a space for themselves and laid the pile of completed questionnaires on the table.

Robin's stomach churned. *He's just coming to pick up Ari*, she told herself over and over. Her stomach, however, kept churning. It wouldn't believe her.

Zo-Zo divided the answered questionnaires into three piles. She handed them each a pencil, and they started marking.

"Jeez, I thought I was bad," Zo-Zo said. "Most of these kids in my pile here are going to need an entire universe to stay alive."

Brodie laughed. "The guy I'm marking needs fourteen other planets already."

Robin grimaced. "Mine are pathetic, too."

"Don't worry," Brodie said. "Their total points *are* going to be bad the first time around. Just like mine were. But then we're giving them our Green Extreme Fact Sheet, and they're all going to turn into *Green Machines!*"

"We wish," Robin said.

Brodie was undaunted. "People *want* to be green, they just need to be told how to do it. You'll see."

Robin looked at Brodie. How did he always manage to be so positive?

A car door shut. Robin tensed. Her father. She wanted him to come in, pick up Ari, and go.

Squirm called from the living room. "Ari, Dad's here."

Ari came down the stairs just as their father opened the kitchen door.

"Hi, everyone," he said pleasantly.

*Phew*, Robin thought. She could feel her shoulders dropping down from her ears.

Her father nodded at Ari. "Meet you in the car." He went back out, and Ari followed.

Robin waited for the sound of the car starting, but it didn't come. She dug the side of her thumbnail into her mouth. She hated chewing her nails in front of people, but she couldn't stop herself. What was her father doing? Her thumb started to bleed.

Zo-Zo waved her hand in front of Robin's face. "Robin to earth. Robin to earth."

Robin looked up and forced herself to concentrate.

Zo-Zo carried on. "I was just saying that —"

The screen door slapped against the house. Robin didn't want to turn around and face her father, but she made herself.

He stood in the doorway, his hands bunched into fists. "What are those skunks doing in the barn? And the squirrels?'

Zo-Zo looked stricken. "I brought the skunks, Mr. Green. It's my fault. My dad and I —"

Her father's stern eyes didn't leave Robin's face. "And you told her it was okay?"

"I didn't know what to do, I —"

"I expressly told you 'no more animals'!" His eyes moved to Zo-Zo. "We don't have the proper enclosures, or food. We aren't licensed."

"There was no place else to take them, Dad, I —"

He looked sternly at Brodie and Zo-Zo. "You two will have to go."

Robin reddened. She *hated* being reprimanded in front of her friends. "But we're working on a school pro —"

His face darkened. "No 'buts'!" His voice was harsh.

Zo-Zo gathered up the contest pages quickly and stuffed them into a bag. She kept her eyes down. Brodie stood as well, his chair scraping across the floor.

"Get into the car," Robin's father said. "I'll drive you both home."

Zo-Zo gave a slow, sad wave to Robin and moved towards the door. Brodie followed, his head down.

"Tell Ari I'll be out in a minute," her father said.

Robin and her father stared at each other. Robin could hardly breathe.

"You disobeyed me."

She nodded. The anguish on his face wrenched her. "I'm sorry, Dad." She hoped her apology would soften him, but it didn't.

"Get in here, Squirm," her dad called into the living room. "I know you're part of this, too."

Squirm crept in, his hands stuffed into the pockets of his baggy jeans.

"Sorry, Dad."

"Both those kids know about the bear now — that's what I'm most worried about. If this gets out, we're going to have the authorities breathing down our necks. We don't need that."

"They won't tell," Robin cried. "We made them promise!"

"And it's only until Mukwa's arm heals," Squirm said. "Then we'll be letting him go."

Their father let out a long breath through his mouth. "All right, but we have to keep this to ourselves. As I said, my boss at the clinic is a real stickler. I don't want to lose my job. We'd have to move again and —"

He swallowed hard, and Robin jumped into the silence, speaking quickly and fiercely "No one's going to find out! I promise. Double promise."

There was a knock at the door.

"Come in," their dad shouted.

Squirm's friend Tommy stepped into the kitchen. He looked at them innocently.

"Wow, I went to see the squirrels. Cool bear. Where'd you get *that*?"

# CHAPTER THIRTEEN

"I'm in hot water too," Griff said when she and Robin were talking over, once again, what had happened.

"Why?" Robin asked.

"Because I knew what you were doing and didn't blow the whistle." She set out a plate of oatmeal cookies and settled back with her tea. "I should have fessed up right at the start and battled it out with your father instead of just not saying anything."

Robin took a cookie and ate all around the edge. She watched it get smaller and smaller. "I don't think he would have given in, no matter what you said."

"Maybe not, but it would have been more honest." Griff looked at Robin. "What about you? Do *you* think what we did was right?"

It felt strange to be asked. Most adults were so busy *telling* you what was right that this wasn't a question she'd ever considered.

"I don't know," she finally said. "It's weird, because it felt right to keep the skunks, but it didn't feel right to hide them. But if I didn't hide them, I wouldn't have been able to keep them."

"Talk about being caught between a rock and a hard place." Griff took a cookie and ate half of it in one bite.

"I don't think I could have turned the skunks away," Robin said. "But I sure hate it when Dad's mad at me." With her mother gone, his anger felt even worse.

Griff chewed the rest of her cookie slowly then pushed the plate away. "Don't let me have any more, even if I beg."

Robin smiled.

Griff brushed the cookie crumbs off her hands. "There was a story on the radio the other day about this kid who got arrested for skateboarding down the main street of his town. The mayor had just announced that the town needed to be more environmental, so the boy was trying to help by propelling himself with his own power instead of going by car or bus. Anyways, the police gave the boy a ticket!"

"Really?"

"Wait, that's not all. The boy refused to pay it, and the police, if you can believe it, threw him in jail!"

Robin felt a rocket of indignation go through her. "Jail? They put him in jail? Is there a jail for kids?"

Griff nodded emphatically. "They have special ones for young people." She stood, took an apple from the bowl on the table, and cut it in half. She wiped the knife on her sleeve. "It gets even better." Her eyes glinted. "When the townspeople found out the kid was in detention, they all started skateboarding down the main streets, too. In protest." She bit into the apple and laughed. "So many people that the town had to change the silly law." She slapped her leg in delight.

"Just goes to show you that anyone, even a kid, can make a difference." Her expression changed. "Sad though — when they interviewed the kid on the radio, he said his mom still wasn't talking to him."

"How come?"

"Guess she was worried he was becoming a trouble-maker. Other people can get awfully squirmy when you go against the rules." Griff nodded towards the photograph of Emmeline Pankhurst. "You think Emmeline's father supported what she did?"

Robin shook her head. Probably not.

"No chance!" Griff popped the rest of the apple into her mouth core and all. "Now don't get me wrong, I'm not saying you shouldn't listen to your dad. You should. But listen to your own heart first."

Griff reached for another cookie. Robin pulled the plate away. Griff lunged and got one anyway. "You got to be fast to beat your granny." She winked.

Robin looked out the window, and her jaw dropped. "The bear's out there! The mother bear!"

As Griff swung around, Robin grabbed the cookie out of Griff's hand. It broke, leaving them both with half.

Griff grinned. "You imp!" She raised the half-cookie in salute. "But don't be making jokes about that mother bear. If she shows up, you won't be laughing, my girl. You won't be laughing at all."

They finished eating in silence.

"Anyways," Griff said, "given your father's feelings, I think we should take a temporary break from rescuing animals. And hope like heck the word doesn't get out about the ones we have."

"Everyone is sworn to secrecy," Robin said. She'd made both Zo-Zo and Brodie swear two more times not to say anything, and Squirm had done the same with Tom. Squirm was the weak link in that he liked to talk, but she planned to keep the pressure on him big time.

Griff looked unconvinced. "Maybe so, but keeping a secret in a small town is like trying to cook pizza and not have it smell. Pretty darn impossible."

"No one else is going to find out," Robin said. She put as much strength as she could into the words, but something niggled inside her. Not until later on that day when she was in bed and just about to go to sleep did she figure out what that niggle was all about. She sat up in bed.

The photographs! What if the photographs Zo-Zo had taken of the animals somehow got into general circulation? Zo-Zo had said she would only show them to Robin and Brodie, but Robin realized now that even that was a risk. She would have to talk to Zo-Zo at school tomorrow and plead with her to erase them from her camera and computer. That was the only way to make sure they were never seen by anyone.

All night she twisted and turned. She talked to Zo-Zo about the photos several times. Then she'd wake up, see that the room was dark and realize she'd been dreaming. Was morning ever going to come?

Finally, the alarm went off. Groaning, she stood up and the room began to spin. She tried to swallow and felt a sharp pain in her throat. When she opened her mouth to speak, no words came out, only a raspy whisper that left her throat feeling as if she were trying to push a toothpick through it.

She dressed anyway and went downstairs. Griff took one look at her and raised her large hand to Robin's forehead.

"Goodness, what are you trying to do, child, burn the house down? No school for you today."

Robin started to protest, but every attempted word scraped her throat like glass.

"Back to bed, sweet girl. I'll bring you some broth later."

That afternoon, spring rains pounded on the roof of the farmhouse. Robin slept fitfully, plagued with crazy dreams. In one of them, someone was chasing her with a camera, but the camera was shaped like a gun, and it fired bullets. She woke up sweating. Pulling herself to sitting, she checked the clock. It was two thirty in the afternoon. Soon Zo-Zo would be home from school. She would call then, but she fell asleep again, and when she awoke, it was early evening. Resolved to call before it was too late, she opened her mouth to ask her brother to bring her the phone, but couldn't make a sound.

Robin's voice didn't return for four days. When it did come back, even though it was weak and squeaky, she told Griff she was going to school.

Griff frowned. "We'll see what the thermometer says." She put the glass tube in Robin's mouth then picked up some clothes and went to put them in the laundry.

The moment Griff's back was turned, Robin slipped the thermometer out of her mouth, only putting it back in when she heard Griff climb the stairs.

Griff squinted as she held the glass tube up to the light then put her hand on Robin's forehead. "You still feel hot, but this darn thing says you're back to normal."

Robin pushed the covers aside and started to dress.

"Don't see why you're so hot to trot about getting back to school." Griff wrapped a wool scarf around Robin's neck. "Didn't think you liked the place."

Robin wondered the same thing as the bus pulled up to the school and she saw Brittany and her gang of friends hanging around the front door. She looked for Brodie but couldn't see him.

The other kids exited the bus, and the driver turned to her. "I haven't got all day."

Robin took a deep breath and got out. Her legs felt wobbly. She didn't feel well, she didn't feel well at all.

Seeing Robin, Brittany elbowed her friends. "Hey, it's skunk girl!"

Robin tried to push past them. Who had told them? Who?

A girl's face thrust itself in front of her. She was pinching her own nose. "Ew! She stinks!"

The other kids copied her, all pinching their noses. Robin put her head down and pushed forward, but the gang pressed into her, stopping her forward motion.

"Ska—unk. Ska—unk!" The kids chanted.

The bell rang, and the grenade of kids exploded in every direction. Robin stood for a moment, not knowing what to do. If only she could go home. Sighing deeply, she forced herself to go into the school. At least now maybe she'd find out who had finked about the skunks. Was the word out about the other animals too?

Zo-Zo ran up to her. "It was a mistake, I —"

Robin's voice was raspy, but she got the words out. "I just got called 'skunk girl' by you know who."

Zo-Zo shoved a finger under her thick glasses and rubbed one of her eyes. Both looked puffy, as if there were a bunch of tears behind the lids just bursting to get out. "It's my fault," she said. "I printed those stupid photos for Brodie, and somehow Brittany got her hands on them."

Mr. Lynch was at his desk now and asking the class to come to order.

"Brodie feels terrible."

Robin turned. Across the class, Brodie was looking at her. His eyes were one long lament.

Feeling woozy, she sat down at her desk. Suddenly, the world felt very slippery and unsafe. She tried to give herself a handrail of hope. Just because a bunch of kids knew didn't necessarily mean her dad would find out, did it?

"As long as my dad doesn't find out, that's all I care about," she whispered to Zo-Zo.

Zo-Zo's lips twitched. "There's more. It's worse. Way worse. I —"

"Quiet!" Mr. Lynch ordered.

He started to teach a geography lesson. Robin sat in her chair feeling so dizzy and fuzzy-headed, she couldn't follow the lesson. What did Zo-Zo mean, "It's worse"? How could things possibly be worse? Various possibilities filled her mind. What if the authorities had been told? Would her family get fined? Would someone come and try to take all the animals away? What if they were taking them away right now while Robin sat in school? She squirmed in her seat and chewed her thumbnails until they bled.

Mr. Lynch droned on and on. Now she wished fervently that she'd stayed home. This was turning out to be the *worst* day of her life. And it wasn't over yet.

When the bell for recess finally sounded, Robin bolted from the classroom, pulling Zo-Zo behind her. She led Zo-Zo around the corner of the school and pushed her against the brick wall.

"Tell me."

Zo-Zo's eyes looked as if they were going to pop out of her head. "Someone sent the photographs to my dad."

Robin was confused. What did Zo-Zo's dad have to do with anything? Then she remembered. Zo-Zo's dad was the editor of the local newspaper.

Zo-Zo gripped Robin's arm as if trying to steady herself. "He didn't know we were trying to keep the animals a secret. So he printed the pictures. They're going to be in today's newspaper."

Robin fell against Zo-Zo.

Now everyone in the entire town would know. In graphic detail. The thing she had feared most had happened.

Robin felt as if she were taking an elevator down into a cold and dark cellar. She put her face in her hands.

Getting herself into trouble was bad enough, getting her dad into trouble was the worst, the very worst.

Zo-Zo winced then pulled her hoodie over her head. It was starting to rain. "Come on. Let's go inside before we get soaked."

Robin hadn't noticed the rain. She let Zo-Zo pull her inside. They went into the cafeteria. As they passed, two kids held their noses.

For the rest of the afternoon, Robin sat at her desk and worried. Mr. Lynch was writing all kinds of things on the board, but she kept her head down, pretending to take notes. Her page was filled however, with only one word. "Stupid." She wrote it and wrote it and wrote it.

She kept staring at the clock. She wanted the school day to be over but dreaded that too. She kept picturing her father and the way his face got splotchy when he was mad.

When the school day finally ended, Zo-Zo turned to her. "Want me to go home with you?"

Robin shook her head. Nothing was going to help now. She pulled up the hood of her coat and started walking.

Zo-Zo stared at her. "You're not taking the bus?"

Robin shook her head and set off. It would take her over an hour to walk, but she didn't care. She was in no hurry to get back. Her father was going to be furious, that she knew. Would he yell at her? Ground her? Keep her in her room for the rest of her life? She wiped her sweaty palms on her jeans and forged onward.

She slowed her steps as she walked up the lane. Her father's car was parked in the driveway. That was not a good sign. Normally he didn't come home until an hour or so after she did. She winced and warily made her way to Griff's. Maybe Griff would be able to tell her how mad her father was. Maybe Griff would go into the farmhouse with her. But Griff was not in her cabin. She must be talking with their dad about how to punish her.

Robin crept towards the house and let herself in the kitchen door. Her father was slumped at the table. Griff was sitting beside him, looking grim. The newspaper was spread out on the table. Even from a few feet away, Robin could see the photo of Mukwa. Beside it were photos of the squirrels and skunks.

Griff and her father turned to see her. Her father's face looked haggard and sad — just as it had the day of her mother's funeral.

She watched as he opened his mouth to speak. She expected his voice to be loud. But it wasn't. In fact, it was so soft she could barely hear it.

When he spoke, he said only three words. At first, Robin didn't think she'd heard them right. They were the worst words ever, and she wanted to shove them back into his mouth. She just stared at him, her jaw falling as he spoke, her eyes wide.

He said the words again. "I got fired."

# CHAPTER
# FOURTEEN

In the days that followed, the house became strangely quiet. It had been like that after her mother had become sick, too, but the quietness then had been sad and damp somehow, like a foggy morning. This time, the quiet was as loud as a scream. And it had a long finger in the middle of it, a finger that was pointed accusingly at her.

Not that her father said anything. He didn't. He just got quiet, deathly quiet. It was Ari who said the words Robin knew everyone was thinking. "If it weren't for you, we wouldn't be in this mess."

Robin had cowered, hearing these words, but Ari was right. It *was* her fault.

Unable to stand how awful she felt around the farmhouse, Robin went to Griff's often and made excuses to go down to the barn. Anything to avoid seeing her father sitting on the porch, hour after hour, staring at the lake, his eyes as lifeless as ashes.

One afternoon when she and Zo-Zo and Brodie were in the library, marking the second round of contest questionnaires, Robin expressed, once again, how guilty she felt.

Zo-Zo looked stricken. "I'm the one to blame. I never should have taken those pictures."

"No, I'm the one to blame," Brodie said. "I'm the one who lost them. I can't believe it. I feel so stupid!"

Zo-Zo rolled her eyes. "Come on, Brodie. You didn't *lose* them. Brittany *stole* them."

A pained expression filled Brodie's face, and he looked away.

Robin was glad they felt badly. She *wanted* them to feel badly.

Brodie turned to Robin. "Do you think your dad's going to be able to find another job?"

Robin shrugged. She didn't think so, based on what she'd heard her father and Griff saying. "Right now, he's not even looking. He's just doing that staring into space thing, big time."

Brodie looked down. "My dad stares into space all the time. But then he's always got a beer in his hand. I can't tell you how many times he's passed out, and I've had to peel his fingers off the bottle."

Robin saw the anguish in Brodie's eyes and wished she could say something wise or helpful, but she didn't know what that would be.

Zo-Zo grimaced. "My mom used to stare into space too. Then she left."

Robin tensed. Her father would never leave them, would he? The word *never* clutched at her throat. She never would have thought her mother would have gotten sick either.

"Come on," Zo-Zo said. "Let's get back to our project." She picked up the next questionnaire. "So, by now, thanks to us, every kid in our school has answered our questionnaire. Twice. Once before reading the 'Green Extreme Factsheet' and once after. Our job today is to see if they made any improvements!"

"Bet they have," Brodie said.

"Oh, I almost forgot." Zo-Zo shoved an envelope into Robin's hands.

"What's this?"

"It came with a letter to the editor supporting the animal shelter," Zo-Zo said.

Robin opened the envelope. Three twenty dollar bills fell out. "Great. Food for the animals." So far, Griff had been paying for all the supplies. Robin liked the idea of being able to help with that.

Brodie looked concerned. "You need money for the animals?" He took a few bills from his pocket. "For the bear … I don't want him to go hungry."

Robin smiled and tucked the bills into a special pocket.

Zo-Zo tapped her pen on the table. "Okay, let's get marking!"

An hour later, they had scored the last questionnaire.

Zo-Zo clicked the pen against her lips. "Now, let's record the second scores and compare them to the first — see if there's a difference."

Brodie beat a drum roll, and they began reading out the score differences for each person.

"Todd Smith, up two points. Courtney Lee, up six — wow! Josh Robbins, up three. Stacie LaFleur up ten! Rachael Conners up eight."

When they were done, Brodie raised his arm in victory. "Wow, every single student got a better score but one."

Zo-Zo cheered. "And some were better by ten or twelve points! That's amazing!"

Brodie grinned triumphantly. "See? We *have* made people change."

Robin smiled despite herself.

"So, who's our winner?" Brodie sounded another drum roll.

Zo-Zo reviewed the list. "It's a tie between Josh Eagan and Christie Parlett."

"But we've only got one grand prize!" Brodie said. "That hundred dollar gift certificate."

"Maybe they can split it," Robin suggested.

The others nodded.

Zo-Zo flipped her notebook to a new page. "Now we'd better make some decisions about the awards assembly. Like who we should get to make the presentation to the winners! My dad says if we get someone important, we'll get more press coverage."

"How about the mayor?" Robin said. "Ed Goodings?"

Brodie frowned. "That's not fair. We're in the middle of an election. If we're going to invite one candidate, we should invite the other."

"Rick Kingshot?" Zo-Zo challenged. "You just refuse to see what a creep that guy is, don't you? Even my dad

142

says he's a slimeball. But then he thinks all lawyers are slimeballs."

Brodie's face hardened. "That's because your mother ran off with one."

Zo-Zo's face spun to one side as if she'd been slapped. When she turned back to them, her face was red. Slowly, loudly, she pushed her chair back and grabbing on to the sides of the desk with both hands, pulled herself up, and strode from the room.

Brodie closed his eyes. He blew air out his mouth so hard, the hair on his forehead shot up. "I shouldn't have said that."

Robin stood up. What was with this boy? He said things when he shouldn't and didn't say things when he should. She picked up her books and stood.

"Wait, I —"

Robin turned towards him. "Wait? Why? So I can listen to you defend Brittany and her dad? I don't think so!" Briskly, she went off in search of Zo-Zo.

All the way home, Robin thought about her two friends. She didn't blame Zo-Zo for running out of the library. What Brodie had said had been mean. Really mean. Was Brodie mean like that because his dad was drunk all the time? Or was he just mad because Zo-Zo had called Rick Kingshot a slimeball. He obviously felt he needed to defend Kingshot. But why? Just because the guy had bought him a bike? People were so complicated.

As she walked up the lane to her house, she heard shouting and stopped.

"It's not fair," Ari was shouting.

Robin edged closer.

"It's got nothing to do with fair," her father shouted back.

"*All* the other kids are going!"

"Ari, it's a *bush* party!" Her father's voice was calmer now. She could hear him restraining himself. "There'll be drinking. And who knows what else. And no parental supervision. You're only fourteen!"

"But I'll be with Conner. He'll —"

"Conner is sixteen, Ari. Sixteen! And from what I've heard, he's not very responsible."

"That's not true. He's the captain of the football team, he's —"

"I don't care of if he's the class president, you're not going!"

Ari made an infuriated huffing sound. "*I hate you!*"

Robin heard her stomping loudly up the stairs. After that, the screen door to the front porch slammed, and Robin knew her father had stormed out to the lakeside porch to get back to his staring place.

She sighed and went inside. Quietly, she went upstairs to change. As she came into the bedroom, she could hear Ari sobbing.

Ari was lying on the bed. She turned quickly so she was facing the wall, but not before Robin had seen the agony on her sister's tear-streaked face.

Robin changed quickly into her barn clothes. Rarely had she seen Ari cry like this. Griff's words about her sister hurting came back to her. Should she say something? She wanted to, but she was scared to as well. What should she say?

She thought about it for a moment, then whispered, "Ari, are you —"

Ari moved closer to the wall, her shoulders hunched high. Just then the phone rang.

Robin turned and bounded for the phone. Her father, however, beat her to it.

His voice was still loaded with anger from his fight with Ari. Robin pitied the person at the other end of the phone.

"No, we are *not* a wild animal shelter."

Robin crept into the kitchen on her way out. Her father was drumming his fingers against the wall. She could tell he was trying to calm himself.

"I know what the article said.... No, we aren't rehabilitating wild animals. No. It was a mistake. No, I don't know where else you can take it." His voice got louder. "Listen, mister, there's nothing I can do."

His face reddened as he listened for a short moment. Then he shouted, "If they euthanize it, it's *not* my problem!"

Robin ran from the house, letting the screen door flap. She let herself into Mukwa's enclosure and sat down. Her heart was pounding.

Griff, who was changing the straw in the puppy enclosure, came towards her. She gazed at her granddaughter through the slats. "You look like you're about to blow a gasket."

"Dad's screaming at someone on the phone again."

"Someone calling about an animal?"

Robin nodded. "Yes."

"He hates turning them down. That's the real problem. He *loves* animals, and I think it's just about killing him not to help," Griff said.

"Then why *doesn't* he help? I mean, the worst has already happened, he's been fired. He can do what he wants now."

Griff took in a big breath, her nostrils flaring. "Beats me. I think he's just so angry about everything, he's like a big inferno. You can't think straight when you've got that much anger inside."

"Before that, he and Ari had a screamer too. You should have heard it."

"I think I did. Part of it, anyways."

"Ari said she hated him."

Griff rubbed her jaw with her hand. "Oh, my!"

"She wants to go to some bush party! He said no."

"Can't blame him. Those parties usually get pretty drunk and disorderly. Besides, Conner is two years older than Ari. His hormones are pushing him hard. I don't know if Ari's old enough to withstand that yet."

Robin wished she understood more about hormones. And why did they blast through teenagers, causing such havoc?

"You should have heard him on the phone. He yelled at the guy."

Griff frowned. "Not good."

"That's all he does lately, scream at people or stare into space."

Griff's frown deepened. "He'll get over it. He'll get back on track. You'll see."

"What if he doesn't?"

Griff smiled gently. "Don't those 'what ifs' drive you crazy? They drive *me* crazy!"

Robin shrugged. It was just what her mind did.

Griff's eyes were soft. "Mukwa will be going back to the wild soon. Then we can all relax. I don't like the way his mom's been prowling around. Makes me nervous. I know it makes your dad nervous too."

Robin stroked Mukwa's ears. "Once he's free, will we ever see him again?"

"Hard to say. But if you do, he'll remember. Bears have great memories."

Robin thought about the mother bear. "What about the mother? What if she remembers? Won't she want to kill me for taking her baby away?"

Griff swatted the air. "Nah! Bears have an uncanny sense of who to trust and who not to trust. I think she'll just be glad to have Mukwa back." She shook her head at the tattered state of Mukwa's cast. "He's sure shredded this thing."

"Why do they put a cast on a broken bone anyway?"

"To keep the bones from moving around. They heal better when they're still. That's what your dad needs, some 'still' time. He's had a lot happen this year." She looked into Robin's eyes. "He'll pull himself together." She broke into a grin. "I'll get Owlie on the case."

Robin scrunched her face doubtfully.

"You think 'cause Owlie's dead, he can't help? He may not have a body, but he has a spirit. A strong spirit."

Robin didn't know what to say, so she remained quiet.

"The Aboriginals say we each have an animal spirit, or what they call a 'totem.' That totem guides us, reminding us who we are." Griff patted her heart. "Not 'who we are' like what your name is, but who you are *inside*."

"Do I have a totem?"

Griff laughed. "I don't think we'd have much trouble figuring that out! I'll give you a clue. Yours is black and has a tail and is trying to teach you about water."

"Relentless?"

"She and I have been chatting about how to get you feeling safe in the water again this summer, haven't we, girl?" Relentless barked from a few enclosures over.

Robin groaned. She couldn't learn to swim if she wasn't willing to go near water, and she wasn't. It was just too scary.

"I can see you're loving that idea," Griff said, tousling Robin's hair. "We'll see when the weather warms up. Meanwhile, don't worry about your dad. He's just pulled in two different directions right now. That logical mind of his is telling him to clear the animals out — after all, we are breaking the law. But there's another part of him that truly wants to help them."

"Last week we had calls about two abandoned birds, a hurt fox, then there was that loon that had a fishing lure wrapped around its leg."

"You're keeping a record of the number of calls, right?"

"Trying to," Robin said. "I've counted thirteen so far! Nobody out there cares about whether we're legal or not, they just want us to help."

"Oh, did you see the paper?" Griff beamed. "There's a letter to the editor actually *supporting* the idea of a wild animal shelter."

"Yeah, Zo-Zo told me. Whoever wrote it sent in a donation."

Griff's eyebrows shot up. "Just goes to show that people *do* support us." She made a thumbs-up sign. "Maybe that'll make your dad feel easier."

"I doubt it," Robin said.

"Like the rest of us, he just doesn't want any more bad stuff to happen. 'Cause when bad stuff happens, it kind of makes you nervous. You know that as well as anybody. I mean, you weren't always afraid of water. Then something happened to get you scared. Want to tell me about it yet?"

Robin nodded. She felt ready now. "I almost drowned."

"When? Not here —"

"In the city. At the pool. Ari and I were fooling around. She pushed me in and I swallowed a bunch of water. I couldn't breathe, I couldn't get myself to the surface, I —" Her palms started to sweat. Remembering was bringing back the panic. "Some lifeguard had to rescue me. They had to give me mouth-to-mouth re ... resus ..."

"Resuscitation?"

"Yeah."

"Sounds awful," Griff said.

Robin pumped her head up and down.

Griff was quiet for a long while. "Bad things happen sometimes. I think that's why your dad's being so careful these days. He just doesn't want any more awfulness."

Robin felt sympathy for her dad. She didn't want any more awfulness either.

"Problem is, once you've had some bad things happen, it's easy to be scared that other bad things are on their way."

"Do you get scared?" Robin asked.

"Sure do. Right now I'm scared this situation with the animals is going to blow up in our faces! Which it could do so fast it would make your head spin. Think about it. We have wild animals without a permit — that's against the law. The town officials aren't going to let us do that forever. I wouldn't be at all surprised if the sheriff shows up on our doorstep one day."

Robin felt her stomach do a cartwheel. "What would happen to the animals?"

The lines on Griff's face tugged at each other, creating deep gashes in her face. Robin had never seen her grandmother look so old and battered. "I'm scared to think."

# CHAPTER FIFTEEN

Robin ran outside in a pair of cut-off jeans and a T-shirt. After a cold, hard winter, it was so freeing to toss off her heavy jacket and boots and feel the freshness of the air slide along her face and arms. There was something so new and irresistible about this time of year. It was hard not to feel happy through and through.

She climbed on top of a huge boulder that over-looked the water. Relentless scrambled up behind her. She liked having the dog by her side again. Now that the puppies were older, Relentless could be away from them for longer periods. In fact, her father said that this was an important part of preparing them for going off on their own. Robin winced at the thought. Why did everything always have to change?

She sat with her back against a tall pine tree that stood regally in the middle of a rock, its long roots going down over the sides to the earth below. She could feel the heat radiating up into the backs of her legs. A light breeze streamed across the lake and fluffed her hair. She pulled the freshness of the air deep into her lungs and surveyed the lake. The ice had been gone for a few weeks now and with the sun's reflection on its surface, the lake looked like a huge silver coin.

She wiggled her toes in her sandals. It wouldn't be long now until summer. She repeated the word wistfully. *Summer*. She couldn't believe it was finally coming. Last summer she'd still been in the city. With her mom. Her mom had been sick, but alive. That time felt so close and yet so far away. How could that be?

It was weird. Sometimes she couldn't even picture her mom any more. Then, at other times, the memories of her would be so sharp, they'd jab into her like darts. That was why she had to keep her guard up, so the darts couldn't go in.

Her thoughts were interrupted by the sound of three Jet Skis charging out into the lake, carving deep grooves into the calm water. All of them had bright yellow flames down the sides, so Robin knew they belonged to the Kingshots.

"And so it starts," Griff said, appearing beside her. She stared at the boats and shivered. "Wouldn't that be a bit cold? Even in wetsuits?"

Robin watched the boats as they made big figure eights in the water. They seemed intent on creating as much commotion on the surface as possible.

"Don't know why they can't play out in the middle of the lake," Griff said. "Away from the loons and ducks — and old people like me who want their peace and quiet." She made a visor of her hand. "Seems like they're at it kind of early this year." She craned her neck forward. "Is that Ari on the back of Conner's Jet Ski?"

"Yup."

"I'm surprised your dad let her."

"They had a big fight about it. Dad finally gave in."

Griff thought for a moment. "Maybe he's trying to make up for saying no to the bush party."

"Maybe. They fight all the time now."

"I fought with my parents, tooth and nail," Griff said. "It's all part of growing up. Ari was acting like she had to protect your dad for a while there — it's good to see her acting like a normal teenager again. Although don't tell your father I said that." She focused her attention on the boats again. "Is that Brodie driving the third one?"

Robin had been trying to figure that out since the boats had appeared. She shrugged. "I don't think Brodie owns a Jet Ski."

"Maybe Kingshot bought him one."

Robin glanced at Griff sharply. "He already bought Brodie a bike."

"I know. You told me. I'm sure Brodie could use someone acting in a fatherly way towards him. Every boy needs that."

Maybe that's why Brodie defended the Kingshots. They had become like a family to him.

Griff sighed. "If it were anyone else, I might think, 'That's nice — there's a man doing something kind for a kid,' but unfortunately, Kingshot only does things that benefit him. Conner, as far as I can see, is no different."

Robin watched as the boats headed out towards Berry Island.

"All Ari talks about is Conner. She, like, calls him twenty times a day."

Griff's face bunched in concern. "That doesn't sound like her."

"I know. Usually the boys are after *her*. Not this time. She's, like, crazy about the guy." All her sister's notebooks were covered with hand-drawn hearts with her and Conner's initials in the centre. It was disgusting.

Griff was quiet for a moment. "A boy like Conner likes the chase. Doubt if he'll stick around if that's not there." She grimaced. "Oh, I hate the thought of Ari getting hurt. She's had so much hurt already." She sucked in some air between her teeth. "But sometimes that's what it takes to wake us up. There's nothing like emotional pain to get us looking at what we're doing."

They watched as the jet skis landed on Berry Island.

"Soon it will be berry picking time," Griff said. "Maybe we can get the whole family to paddle out there and pick some."

*No way*, Robin thought. The closest she was going to get to water was the dock.

Griff shook her head. "What gets me is that Kingshot is in the middle of an election campaign, but he's out there boating. Meanwhile, his opponent, Ed Goodings, is working himself to the bone for every vote. I'm going canvassing for Ed this week to help him out."

A car honked. Griff stood up wearily. "Guess peace and quiet is not on the agenda today." The car honked again. "Okay, okay, we're coming." She offered Robin a hand up. "Come on, let's go and see who's making all that racket."

Robin followed Griff up to the farmhouse. There was a red car in the driveway. Who did they know that had a red car? No one she could think of.

"Who the heck's that?" Griff wiped her hands down the sides of her jeans.

A small boy got out of the car. He was carrying a cardboard box.

"Uh-oh," Griff said. "A cardboard box can only mean one thing!"

Robin didn't know what kind of animal was in the box, but she was certain it contained one. "Dad will yell at them, you watch."

"Maybe we can head them off at the pass. Come on."

As Robin and Griff approached, a woman got out of the driver's seat. "Is this the wild animal shelter?"

Griff opened her mouth to speak, but her son shot out the farmhouse door.

"*No!* This is *not* a wild animal shelter!" A vein in his temple throbbed.

The boy put the box on the ground and was about to open it, "We have a hurt —"

Robin's dad cut him off. "I don't care *what* you have. Take it somewhere else."

"But he's bleeding," the boy said, his lower lip wobbling.

Another boy got out of the car. He was about fifteen. "Look, mister, just take a look, will you?"

Robin's dad took a step towards the box but stiffened and stopped. "I don't want to look. If it's bleeding, you should take it to a vet."

"You *are* a vet," Griff said simply. "Have you forgotten?"

"You're a vet?" The woman's eyes widened with hope.

He nodded. "I am, or was. I —"

The woman looked at him. "We were told you would *help!*"

Robin watched the Adam's apple in her father's throat go up and down.

"It's an owl," the boy said. "Just a little one —" Tears were spilling from his eyes.

"An owl?" Robin's dad sank to his knees. He gently pulled back one of the box flaps.

Robin leaned in. The bird was just a baby, but it had huge, unblinking yellow eyes that were riveted on her father.

He stared and said in a hushed voice. "It's a great horned, just like ..."

"Owlie," Griff said quietly.

Robin watched as the doctor in him took over. Within ten minutes, he had a temporary surgery set up in the barn and was pulling on a pair of plastic gloves. He threw a pair at Robin.

"Okay, girl, put your money where your mouth is. I'm going to need help."

Robin ran to wash her hands. She smiled. The fire was back in her father's eyes.

A few hours later, while the owl lay in recovery, Griff brought a tray with a teapot and several mugs out to the porch. She began to fill the cups. "It's lemon and ginger tea. I think you'll like it." She passed a cup to the younger boy, Ben, then turned to the fifteen-year-old. "How about you, Josh, would you like some?"

The boy nodded.

When everyone had a cup, Griff shouted into the house. "Ari! Come and join us,"

Ari, who had returned a while ago, breezed onto the porch. She was wearing a tight pair of white Capri pants and a top that covered just a little more than a bra. The fifteen-year-old boy looked at her and sat up straighter.

"Ari, this is Josh," Griff said. "And his younger brother, Ben."

Ari glanced at them briefly then stared down the driveway. "I'm just waiting for Conner."

Her father looked at her sternly. "You just saw him. What about your homework?"

Ari looked at her father innocently. "Don't worry, Dad. I need a book from the library to get it done. Conner's taking me. I won't be long."

The woman who had brought the owl raised her cup. "Here's to you, Gord. For saving the owl." Her eyes were bright with admiration.

Robin watched her father blush.

"That owl's lucky. He's definitely going to live. He may have trouble flying again, we'll have to see."

They all turned as a car sped up the driveway.

"Someone should get his muffler fixed," Griff said, grimacing at the noise.

Conner braked hard, and the car lurched to a stop. He flicked a small cigarillo into the bushes.

Griff's eyes widened. "He *smokes*?"

"Not really," Ari said quickly, getting up.

"What's 'not really' about what he just tossed into the bushes?"

Her answer was the sound of Ari's shoes clacking down the wooden porch steps.

Squirm turned to his dad, who was watching Conner and Ari speed away. "What if the baby owl *can't* fly? What will happen to it then?"

Robin waited for her father to jump in with his lecture about no more animals. She watched him thinking. Maybe he didn't want to lecture them in front of company. Parents were like that.

"We'll keep him," he finally said. "I'm sure Owlie would love the company."

"Yay!" Squirm cheered.

The mother stood up. "Thank you *so* much."

"You're welcome," Robin's father said.

Suddenly both boys were pumping her father's hand and everyone was grinning.

"Can we come and see him?" Ben asked.

"Of course!" When the family was in the car, he added cheerily, "Check in with us in a few days to see how he's doing."

When the car had disappeared, he turned to Griff.

"It sure felt good to be working again," he said.

Griff's eyes met his. "I can imagine. Caring for animals is who you are!"

He nodded. "Now all I need is someone to pay me for it."

With sudden zeal, Griff slapped some money into her son's hand.

He stared down at it. "What's this?"

"What's it look like? Money, honey!"

He whistled.

"The woman slipped it to me when you weren't looking."

He counted it. "She didn't have to give us this much!"

Robin ran and got the donation money Zo-Zo had given her. "Here's some more!"

Griff grinned. "See? You *are* getting paid."

Robin's father jerked up his hands. "This won't buy groceries!"

"It *will* buy groceries," Griff countered. "Some, anyway. Besides, there are lots of people out there with hurt animals who will pay you."

"Yes, but we're not licensed to keep the wild ones —"

Robin turned to Griff. She was sick of hearing about this license business. "Can't we just get one?"

"We can try," Griff said. "If your father agrees." She waited for her son to reply, but he just looked away and shifted his weight from one foot to the other. She gripped his arm. "Gord, don't get your knickers in a knot. Everything will work out. We just don't see how yet, but it will. You'll see. Have faith."

His voice was suddenly loud and demanding. "Faith? After all I've been through? Where would I find that?"

Griff's eyes rested on him calmly. "It finds you. But you have to let it."

# CHAPTER SIXTEEN

Suddenly all of nature seemed to be bursting with aliveness. Each morning the birds chirped with such strength and ferocity that Robin couldn't sleep past dawn. And each evening, the frogs that Griff called "peepers" thronged so loudly they kept her up for hours. Out in the fields, water gushed up through the ground, and streams appeared out of nowhere, gurgling their way down to the lake. And the sky sang with a blue so bright it made Robin's heart swell.

In the city, when spring arrived, it was barely noticeable. But here in the country, the sounds and smells and colours were so loud and strong and vivid, it made Robin's head spin. She felt dizzy with the delight of it. She didn't even mind the loudest and most pervasive sound of all: their telephone, which hadn't stopped ringing since the day they'd taken in the baby owl.

How people found out about her dad's change of mind, Robin had no idea. It was as if the animals had run from house to house, whispering in people's ears, for almost overnight they started getting dozens of calls.

Now, instead of turning people and their hurt animals away, Robin's father told everyone the same thing: "Sure, bring it in."

Within days, they'd added five baby raccoons, two ducklings, and a one-year-old bear to the animals already in their care. The bear had suffered multiple cuts trying to break through a window to get some pies a woman had left cooling in her sunroom.

"Will Mukwa be this big when he's a year old?" Robin asked as she watched her father stitch up the sedated bear.

"Bigger, probably, given the size of his mother." He gave the animal a shot of antibiotics, and they took it back to a cage next to Mukwa's. "By the way, I saw Muk's mom again yesterday. Across the field. So be careful. We have another week or so before I'm going to take off the cast and let him loose."

A few days later, they were able to release the other new bear back to the wild.

"Good thing," Griff said. "We can sure use the space with all these babies coming in."

Robin cleaned out the enclosure right away to make room for some baby birds. Every inch of the barn was full of the quacking, barking, mewing, chirping, and sometimes whimpering animals, most of which were babies. Why babies got themselves into so much trouble, Robin didn't know, but they did. Baby birds fell out of nests, baby ducks got caught in boat propellers, baby deer got injured by cars — there seemed to be an endless list of predicaments they got themselves into.

When Robin had the enclosure clean, she settled the baby birds in there and fed them. Then she wrote down what she'd done on a clipboard and attached it to the front of the enclosure. Later her father would add his treatment notes and the expected date of release. He wanted everyone to remember their goal: to heal the animal or bird as quickly as possible and get it back to the wild.

Robin went to the farmhouse to get some apples for Mukwa and found Griff and her dad sitting at the kitchen table. Griff sorted through a pile of mail then tossed the bunch to the side.

"Those people are as slow as molasses," Griff said.

"Who's slow as molasses?" Robin asked.

"Government people. We sent in that application about becoming a proper rehab place and still haven't heard back. Hell's probably going to freeze over first."

"At least we've got it in," Robin's father said. "Now maybe the town will stay off our back."

"That, my dear son, would presume that one government body tells another what it's doing. Not a likely prospect."

"And you call *me* cynical." He smiled.

The phone rang and Griff picked it up. "A goose? With an arrow in its neck? My goodness. Where?" She began writing.

Robin's dad picked up his medical bag and jerked his head towards Robin. "Get your water boots and help me with this one, will you?"

Robin snatched the directions from Griff, ran to get her boots, and beat him to the car. She loved it when she got to do a rescue with her dad.

Griff climbed in the back seat. In her hands she had a hand-made sign and a hammer. "Give me a lift down to the road, will you? I want to put this sign up."

Her son looked at her worriedly through the rearview mirror. "Isn't that pushing it, Mom?"

"It's just a sign. I don't want anyone taking a hurt animal to the Kingshots' by mistake."

"Good point." He pulled over at the end of the road.

Robin looked behind her as they drove off and saw Griff hammering the sign up against a tree. It said THE WILD PLACE. Robin smiled. She liked that name.

"So, where are we headed?" her father asked.

Robin read out the directions, and they sped along the back roads until they came to a mailbox that said "Smith." They kept going until they saw a pond on the left.

"It's supposed to be in there somewhere," Robin said.

Her father pulled his waist-high waterproofs over his pants. Robin was going to have to make do with her rubber boots.

They headed towards the pond and soon saw a goose eyeing them nervously.

"I thought it was supposed to have an arrow in its neck," Robin said.

"That one'll be around here somewhere," her dad replied. "This one here came down to help out the hurt one. That's what geese do. If one's in trouble, another comes to help." He peered through a mass of bulrushes. "Okay, there's the hurt one."

Robin followed his gaze and took in a sharp breath. A goose was standing several yards away with a long arrow skewering the middle of its neck. She swallowed hard. That would hurt.

"Okay, kiddo, your job is to keep that helper goose away from me. I don't want it coming after me while I'm trying to get the hurt one. But whatever you do, don't get close. Their beaks can kill." He thought for a moment. "Wait, I've got a high-tech tool in the car that will help you do that." Moving cautiously so as not to alarm the goose, he went back to the car and returned with a baseball bat. He handed it to Robin.

Robin rolled her eyes at his humour but was glad to have the bat. She could use it to nudge the goose away if it got too close. Keeping her eyes riveted on the goose, she eased her way between it and her dad and started to coral it further away from the hurt one. It paced and made angry noises but backed off.

When she thought she'd manoeuvred it a safe distance away, she snuck a glance back at her dad. He was holding a blanket like a matador and approaching the hurt goose. When he was close, he threw the blanket over its head and grabbed it. Quickly, he gave it a needle, and the bird dropped to the ground.

Robin helped carry it back to the car. Up close, it looked huge. "Can't you just take the arrow out here and set it free?"

"I could, but I'd worry about infection. I want to make sure it's going to be okay."

Robin nodded. "It's not going to be easy finding space for it. We hardly have any cages left."

Her father nodded. "We'll let it sleep with Ari tonight."

Robin laughed. She liked it when her dad made jokes. It was like the good old days.

When they got back to the barn, Zo-Zo was there helping Griff clean some of the cages.

"The only one we didn't do was Mukwa's. I'll leave that one for Brodie." Zo-Zo said. "I know he likes to do that one himself. He's coming today, right?"

Robin nodded. She was glad the three had been able to move past their little upset. Brodie had apologized to Zo-Zo for what he'd said about her mother, and Zo-Zo and Robin had agreed to let mayoralty candidate Rick Kingshot be a part of the upcoming awards assembly, so all was well between the three of them. At least for the moment.

When the day they had so diligently planned for finally arrived, the three sat on the makeshift stage that had been set up at the front of the gymnasium.

They watched as the other students, teachers, and parents came streaming in.

"Jeez, I've never seen the gym so full," Zo-Zo said, squirming in her seat.

"That's because all the parents are here." Brodie frowned. "Except for mine."

*Or mine*, Robin almost said. She didn't have "parents" in the plural at all.

"Isn't that your mom? There, in the corner?" Zo-Zo pointed.

"Oh, yeah," Brodie said, brightening.

"There's my dad!" Zo-Zo waved to a large man who was holding a camera and snapping pictures of them. "He's going to put us on the front page."

"Wow!" Robin said. The word barely came out, her mouth was so dry. She wished they didn't have to be on stage. It was nerve-wracking being up there with everyone staring at them. Then she saw her dad and Griff. They took seats in the very front row. Her dad turned to speak to various people, but Griff caught Robin's eyes and held her gaze. Robin felt Griff's reassurance pouring into her, and she started to relax.

The principal arrived with the mayor Ed Goodings and Rick Kingshot and called the assembly to order. He started by telling the audience about The Big Fat Footprint contest and took a moment to praise Robin, Zo-Zo, and Brodie's ingenuity for thinking up the idea and putting so much effort into making it work. Then he called up the two contest winners and let Rick Kingshot and Ed Goodings award them their prizes. There was a huge round of applause.

When that was done, he called out the names of the runners-up, and Robin, Brodie, and Zo-Zo stepped forward and gave each one a T-shirt. The shirts were all white but had a big green footprint in the middle. When Robin walked across the stage, her knees were so wobbly, she was worried her legs were going to collapse under her.

After the assembly, Peter Donnelly, Zo-Zo's dad, took pictures of Rick and Ed with the winners. Rick kept waving at people and shaking hands with anyone he could.

Zo-Zo, who was watching him, elbowed Robin. "Look at him working the crowd. Pretending to be Mr. Nice Guy. What a faker. My dad says he's spending so much money on his campaign, he might as well just buy the votes outright."

When the group shot was done, Ed Goodings asked Zo-Zo's dad to take a photo of him with Robin.

"You're doing good work with that wild place of yours," he said. He smiled for the camera. "If I'm elected, you can count on my support. Big time!"

"Wild Place! I call it the *wuss* place," Rick Kingshot said, jumping in. "My friend the sheriff wanted to shut it down, but I talked him out of it. Brodie here likes the place." Rick put his hand on Brodie's shoulder and flashed a white-toothed smile at the reporter. "He's my daughter's boyfriend, so I indulge him." He tousled Brodie's hair.

Robin wondered whether Brodie was going to say he wasn't Brittany's boyfriend, but he didn't. But he did do something else that Robin found surprising. He flinched when Mr. Kingshot touched him.

If Mr. Kingshot noticed, he gave no sign of it. He checked his large, shiny watch and left.

"Peter Donnelly," Zo-Zo's dad said, introducing himself to Robin and Brodie. "Can you three squish yourselves together so I can get a cover photo?"

"I feel like a star," Brodie said as he arranged himself between the two girls. He put his arms around them both.

"You *are* a star," Mr. Donnelly said. "You've done something important here." He eased the three of them closer together. "Okay, Brodie, squeeze those gorgeous girls in close. Pull them right in."

Robin suppressed a big smile. She liked being squeezed in closer to Brodie.

The next day, on the driveways and porches of nearly every house in town, Robin, Brodie, and Zo-Zo could be seen grinning from the front page of the newspaper.

"Uh-oh," Zo-Zo said, staring at the photograph. Robin craned her neck over Zo-Zo's shoulder. "You and I are looking at the camera, but Brodie is looking at you! Whoa. His eyes are like, all gooey!"

"No way!" Robin said, but even she could see the almost adoring look in Brodie's eyes. She felt as if someone had lit a sparkler in her chest.

Zo-Zo put the paper down. "Big Brat will have steam coming out her ears when she sees this." She sighed. "Mr. Kingshot isn't going to like it either. Remember what he said? About stopping the sheriff from shutting The Wild Place down?" She looked at Robin with wide eyes. "Once he sees who Brodie *really* likes, he's not going to protect The Wild Place any more. In fact, my guess is he's going to try and get rid of us."

Robin gulped. Having Brittany mad at her was bad enough. Having someone as powerful as Brittany's father mad at her was downright scary.

Zo-Zo blinked nervously. She was obviously having some of the same thoughts. "Now, not only do we have the Big Brat hating us but the Big Bully too."

For the next few days, Robin and Zo-Zo made sure they were never out of sight of the teacher on yard duty or alone in the halls.

"She's going to do something to get us," Zo-Zo said. "Just you wait."

Robin agreed. The only question was *what?* Beat them up? Call them names? Steal more of their homework?

"As long as it doesn't involve The Wild Place," Robin said to Zo-Zo.

"I dare her to even come close to the place," Zo-Zo said indignantly.

"Yeah, but her brother, Conner, comes and picks my sister up all the time," Robin said. She thought back to having seen him flick his smoking cigarillo into the bushes that day he'd picked up Ari. All he'd have to do is flick one into the barn, and the place would ignite like a pile of dry tinder. The barn would become a raging inferno in moments. She shut her eyes, but images of the animals burning in their enclosures made her shudder.

"I'm going to start sleeping in the barn," Robin told Zo-Zo the next morning while they were waiting in class for Mr. Lynch to arrive. "At least on weekends. That way I can hear if anyone comes close."

"But then if there was a fire, you could get burned to death too!" Zo-Zo said. She elbowed Robin. "Don't look now, but you-know-who is coming our way."

Brittany was making her way around the classroom, stopping at each desk and handing out white envelopes.

"For my birthday bash," she said. "There's going to be a band and everything." When she got to Robin's desk, she stopped. "I have one for each of my friends. Since you aren't a friend, you don't get one." She moved on and placed the next invitation on Zo-Zo's desk.

Zo-Zo picked it up and handed it back. "I don't want it."

Mr. Lynch strode into the room, and Brittany went back to her desk. For the rest of the day, the class buzzed with the details of the upcoming party. When the bell finally rang, Robin grabbed her things and left the class quickly. All the way home, she had to listen to the other kids talk about what they were going to wear to the party and what fun it was going to be.

That night, Robin felt more restless than ever. Since it was Friday, she and Griff made pizza, and after dinner, she and Squirm played cards. Ari watched and did her nails.

In the middle of one of their games, their dad announced, "Griff and I are going to the city tomorrow. We need cages." He winked at Robin. It was Griff's birthday the following weekend, and she knew he wanted to get something special for her party, which was on the same weekend as Brittany's. Robin was happy about that. At least she would have *something* to do that night.

He put his hand on his eldest daughter's arm. "Ari's in charge. She's got an exam on Monday, so she's going to be here studying all day. Do what she says, okay?"

Ari smiled sweetly.

Squirm groaned loudly. Robin groaned inwardly.

Robin stayed up and played a few more rounds of cards with Squirm. Finally, when she couldn't stop yawning, she went upstairs. Ari was sitting on her bed with a large magnifying mirror propped on her knees and a pair of tweezers in her hand. She was plucking her eyebrows.

Robin changed into her pajamas and pulled out her book. As she read, Ari applied whitening strips on her teeth. After that, she gave herself a pedicure. What was she up to? There was no way a person primped like that before a day of hitting the books.

Robin turned out her light and pulled her pillow over her head to block out Ari's light. She could hear scribbling. Her sister was writing in her diary, something she often did before going to sleep. Robin was almost asleep when she heard the rustle of covers and finally the light was turned off.

Sometime in the night, the dream grabbed her. It always started the same way. She was plunging down and down into the cold water. No matter how much she kicked and tried to thrust herself up, she could do nothing to stop herself from plummeting into the lake's murky depths.

When she broke into wakefulness, she was panting. Her heart pounding, she fumbled for the light and clicked it on. Ari grumbled in her sleep then turned away, her back to Robin and the night table between them. Too shaken to go back to sleep, Robin dug her arms through the sleeves of a ratty terrycloth robe and crept downstairs. She made herself a cup of hot chocolate, putting two heaping spoons of the chocolate powder into the cup instead of one, and ate digestive cookies while she waited for the milk to heat up. The kitchen clock said four thirty.

Hot chocolate in hand, she went back to bed and propped herself up against the pillows. She sipped her hot chocolate and looked around the room, still feeling unsettled.

Her eyes landed on the diary. It had slipped out from under the pillow and was lying inches from Ari's back. Before Robin could stop herself, she had it in her hand. It was about the size of a thick paperback book. The cover was made of some shiny pink material. In the middle was a small brass lock. Ari wore the key on a chain around her neck, so there was never any possibility of sneaking a look at what was inside.

But there was something funny looking about the lock. Something was off kilter. As Robin stared at it, she realized that the two parts of the lock were not fully fitted into each other. She gave the clasp a slight tug and was amazed when the strap fell open.

Alarmed, Robin looked over at her sister to make sure she was asleep. If Robin was caught doing what she was doing, she would be dead meat.

She opened the book to the most recent entry.

*He can't stop me. I'll sneak out. I won't miss the party! I WON'T!*

The words were written in large, bold letters. What was she talking about? The bush party?

"Turn out the light," Ari said, still facing the wall.

Robin eased the diary shut and clicked off the light. She waited until she could hear the rhythmic sound of Ari's breathing again then slipped the diary back under her sister's pillow.

She lay in the dark, her eyes wide. Was Ari really going to sneak out and go to the bush party? Should she tell her dad? Or Griff? But if she did tell, Ari would know she'd read the diary. And Ari would make her life miserable.

Robin closed her eyes and let sleep take her.

The next thing she knew, Griff was sitting on the end of her bed. Robin yawned and looked outside. The sky was pink as the day dawned.

"You sure you kids are going to be all right, here by yourselves?" Griff rubbed her jaw with her large palm. She shook her head. "I've just got this skittery feeling...."

"Ready when you are, Mom!" Robin's dad called from downstairs.

Robin shut her eyes. The word "mom" still took her breath away.

"Coming." Griff pulled herself up as if her body weighed a thousand pounds. "Be careful, okay? No shenanigans. No wandering around in the woods — that mother bear's still around. And don't let Squirm either. And do what your sister says." She kissed Robin's forehead. "I'll make sure your dad takes his cell phone. See you tonight."

When she was gone, Robin slipped down under the covers. What good was her father's cell phone when he never had it charged?

# CHAPTER SEVENTEEN

Robin's room was bright with sunshine when she woke up for the second time. Knowing the animals would be clamouring for food, she dressed quickly, had some cereal, and went to the barn. The puppies were bigger now, and their hungry yapping was so noisy she decided to feed them first, just to get some quiet. Then she set the food out for Mukwa, who was playing on his swinging tire. As soon as the bowl touched the ground, he gobbled it up quickly. Did animals taste things? Here in the shelter, all the animals got the same thing, meal after meal, yet they always acted as if that particular food was their favourite delicacy.

When Mukwa was finished eating, he kept nudging her.

"Oh, I know what you want," she said, pulling a small ball from one of her coat pockets. She'd brought it in yesterday for Mukwa to play with, and he'd remembered. It was true what Griff said about bears having great memories.

"Bright boy," she said, rolling it to him.

Even in the short time they'd had him, Mukwa had grown bigger. And smarter. He knew his name and lots of other words, Robin was sure of it. She tossed the ball to him over and over, and even though his arm was still in a cast, he caught the ball easily. She loved being with him. It felt like a kind of privilege. After all, how many people ever got to be close to a baby bear? Besides, he was due to be released any day now, and she wanted as much time with him as she could get.

After a good long play with Mukwa, she went on to feed the others. The goose was gone now, its neck completely healed, but they still had raccoons, squirrels, rabbits, and skunks. As always with the adult birds and animals, she kept her distance.

"We want to keep wild things wild," her father had told her over and over again. "If they get friendly with you in here, they'll be friendly with others humans once they're released. People aren't used to wild animals being friendly. They might think the animal has rabies and shoot it."

That thought made Robin keep her distance from all the adult animals and birds. The babies, however, were a different matter. As Griff always said, "Babies are babies. They need love. Lots of love. So give them all you've got."

Robin did. She found there was nothing more satisfying than holding a tiny baby in her arms and feeding it. She didn't know why it made everything else all right, but it did.

She had just finished feeding the rabbits and was putting fresh straw in their enclosure when Squirm appeared. He was still in his pajamas, the ones with the dragonflies all over.

"You ever going to take those off?" Robin asked.

Griff had given him the pajamas a few weeks ago, and Robin didn't think he'd taken them off since. He even wore them under his jeans when he went to school.

"Want me to help with the pup —" He sneezed then sneezed again.

Robin stopped what she was doing and listened to his breathing. There was a faint wheezing sound, she was certain. What if he had a full-blown asthma attack today when her dad and Griff weren't there? She'd already checked to make sure his inhaler was on the fridge, but still, once he'd had such a bad attack they'd had to take him to the hospital. But that was when they'd lived in the city. He hadn't had one attack here in the country. She should have been comforted by that thought, but then another one knocked that one right out of the ball park. What if that meant a huge one was on its way?

Deciding that she'd better get Squirm to stay in the house and be quiet, she said, "Isn't that Spider Boy movie on this afternoon?"

"You'd let me watch that?" Usually they weren't allowed to watch television in the middle of the day.

"Just this once."

"But what about Ari? She'll want that stupid show of hers."

Ari came up to them from behind. "I won't tell Dad about the Spider Boy movie if you don't tell him I'm going to study at the library."

Squirm nodded eagerly, but Robin said nothing. *Yeah, the library. Sure.*

Ari shrugged. "Okay, tell. I don't care. Dad will believe me anyway. He always does."

Conner's car roared up the driveway.

Squirm covered his ears. "When's that stupid boyfriend of yours going to get his muffler fixed?"

"What about your exam?" Robin shouted over the noise. Once upon a time getting good marks had been important to Ari. But obviously not to this girl who was acting like a drop-in from another planet.

Ari shrugged.

Conner was beside them now, a cigarillo in his mouth.

Robin tensed. All she wanted was to get him out of there before he started a fire and burned the place down.

"Hey," he said, standing in front of Mukwa's cage. "How's my little bear rug?"

Robin hissed at Ari, "If you want me to keep my mouth shut, get Conner out of here. Now!"

Ari stiffened her back and turned. "Come on, Conner. Let's go."

Squirm waved the air and started coughing.

"He's allergic," Ari said as she left the barn. Conner followed.

Squirm watched the car race down the driveway, then scampered up to the house. Robin went back to her chores. She finished putting fresh straw in two enclosures and had just started mucking out the raccoon cage when Josh and Ben rode up on their bikes to see the baby owl. Owlie the Second, as he'd been nicknamed, was able to fly but only very short distances. Robin's dad was still hoping he'd heal enough to be released and soar into the skies as nature intended.

Josh and Ben visited with the owl for a while then helped take all the puppies out for a walk. When they were putting the puppies back in their enclosure, Josh looked towards the farmhouse.

"Is Ari around?"

Robin sighed. She knew that look. It was the same look so many boys got when they liked her sister.

"No. She's off with her idiot boyfriend."

Josh looked disappointed. "Tell her I said hi."

"I will," Robin said as she waved goodbye. Now why wasn't Ari interested in a boy like that, she wondered as she returned to her cleaning.

It was a hot day and very still. The animals seemed unusually quiet. In the heat of the afternoon, Robin took a short break and sat in the barn on a bale of hay. She was wiping the sweat from her forehead when she heard a strange sound. She tensed and grabbed the pitchfork. The mother bear? She craned her head around the barn door.

"Brodie!" She dropped the pitchfork, hoping he hadn't seen it.

Brodie set his bike down and ran towards her. "They're coming!" he shouted, his arms flailing.

She could tell from his agitation that something was wrong, very wrong. "Who? Who's coming?"

"To close the place, you've got to —"

This time, she blasted the word at him. "*Who?*"

"The sheriff!" Brodie was standing in front of her now, his hands moving like startled birds. "Mr. Kingshot had the sheriff in his office — I had to press my ear to the door, but I heard them talking." He took a hurried breath and carried on. "The sheriff, he's coming to clear the animals out — *today!* I ran here to tell you, if Mr. Kingshot finds out, I'll be fired but —"

Robin cut him off. "But we've got our application for a license in and —"

"It doesn't matter. You don't have one *now*. I heard the sheriff say that."

"But there's no place to take them!" Robin started to pace. "That means they're going to put them to sleep. Euthanize them!"

Brodie stared at her with astonishment. "Mukwa? *No!* " He smashed his fist into the side of the barn. "Ow!" He jumped up and down, holding his hand.

Robin straightened her back. "We have to stop them."

"But we *can't!* It's the *sheriff*, he's like the police, he's —"

"I don't care!"

"He'll have a gun!"

Robin felt her whole body start to freeze up. Soon she wouldn't be able to move at all. She forced herself to pace. She needed to keep moving.

Brodie's eyes were wild. "Let's open the cages. Let them go. Let them make a run for it."

Robin's mind raced through this possibility. The animals were there because they needed care. It would hurt them to be without that care. Some of them might survive, but others wouldn't. They had to keep them here and protect them. But how? She jammed her thumb between her teeth and tried to think.

Brodie's eyes were desperate. "There's nothing we can do!"

Robin pounced on his words. "We have to try! It's just like the eco thing. Remember, I wanted to give up and you told me that we had to keep trying. And we did. And we figured out what we could do, we —"

Brodie cut her off. "But Kingshot is powerful, he's —"

"I don't care! I have to *do* something!" She pulled herself up straighter. Saying those words made her feel stronger somehow.

Brodie stared at her fiercely, his face white. He swallowed hard then checked his watch. "I've got to get back. Before they figure out what I've done." He turned and hopped on his bike. In seconds, he was gone.

Stunned, Robin watched him go. How could he leave her like this? With the sheriff on his way? But there was a more pressing question pounding her brain: what was *she* going to do? She had to figure out a plan, and she had to figure it out fast.

Breaking into a run, she headed towards the house. She'd phone her father and Griff. They would know what to do. Halfway there, she stopped. What if her father told her to do nothing? She couldn't stand that. Confusion overwhelmed her. She swayed from side to side, uncertain about what to do.

She went to Griff's. The moment she was inside Griff's cabin, she felt herself calm. With shaking fingers, she called Zo-Zo's number. It took her three tries to get the right numbers punched in. The phone rang once. Twice. Then three times. When Zo-Zo's voicemail came on, Robin gushed her message into it.

"Zo-Zo, come quickly. The sheriff is on his way — the animals, they could be —" The voicemail clicked off. Had it even taken her message?

Now what? Think, Robin, think! The sheriff would be arriving any moment. What if she tried to talk to him, what if she tried to explain about the animals needing care.

*He's not going to listen!* a voice inside her harped. *No one's going to listen to a twelve-year-old!*

Her eyes shot up to the gun. With a gun, she could *make* him listen. With a gun, the sheriff would take her seriously. He'd have to. She reached up and took the gun down from the rack. It was heavy in her hands, and the metal felt cold. And mean. This gun had killed things. It had spilled blood. She wasn't planning to shoot anyone but knew the gun would scare them off. That's all she wanted. But what if her fingers slipped on the trigger?

"Put it away," Griff said quietly.

Robin knew the voice belonged to her imagination, but she also knew this was exactly what Griff would say. And that Griff was right.

She eased the gun back up on the rack, and relief flooded through her. But now what? Her eyes cast about the room desperately and stopped on the photograph of Emmeline Pankhurst. The woman's blazing eyes bored right into her.

"What should I do?" Robin whispered aloud.

To her surprise, Emmeline told her. Not in words of course, but like an instant message that went from the suffragette's brain to hers. And she decided right then she was going to take that advice. It was risky, dangerous even, but it was the right thing to do.

She left the cabin and took Relentless to the farmhouse. She didn't want the dog getting hurt. This way, she'd have both the dog and her brother out of the way.

Squirm glanced up. "The movie's great. Want to watch the rest with me?"

"Sure," she said. "I'll just take care of some people who are coming."

Squirm nodded, his gaze staying on the TV. He was used to people coming and going.

Determined now, Robin went outside. Her stomach felt like a gymnasium full of bouncing balls. She busied herself with the animals.

She was cleaning the skunk cages when she heard the sound of tires coming up the driveway. She stopped what she was doing and listened. Most of the people who came to the animal shelter drove cars or vans, and their tires made light, gravelly sounds as they approached. This vehicle sounded heavy, its weight grinding against the gravel as it went.

She peeked through the slats of the barn and saw the sheriff's black pick-up truck approaching. It had a large trailer hitched to the back. The trailer had been brought along to take away the animals. *Of course*, she thought. *He wouldn't put them to sleep here. He'll take them somewhere to do it. If* she let him. But her plan was to stop him. No matter what. It was up to her now. The lives of the animals were in her hands. Fear clawed through her body. She felt shaky, but she got into position anyway.

# CHAPTER EIGHTEEN

By the time the big black truck stopped in the yard, Robin was prepared. She had shut the barn door tightly behind her from the outside, making sure the long bar that went across the whole front of the door was firmly closed. She leaned back now and felt the solid strength of the barn itself. In the stillness, she could smell the hay and the tangy aroma of the various animals. Usually, the animals made some sort of noise — grunting, licking, clawing, yipping, but at the moment, they were dead silent. Griff had told her once that animals were always the first to know about hurricanes, earthquakes, and other natural disasters. They were certainly sensing danger now.

Robin stared into the cab of the black truck. Two men were sitting in the front seat. Both were staring at her. One had leaned so far forward, his nose was almost squashed against the windshield.

Although she couldn't hear them, she could see their mouths moving, and every once in a while, the pointer finger of the man in the passenger seat jabbed the air in front of him. What were they saying? Were they figuring out how they were going to arrest her? Would they use handcuffs? She felt so small leaning up against the barn. And vulnerable. Then she heard them laugh. It was the kind of laugh one of the bullies at school might make if a puny kid challenged him. That startled her.

The sheriff and his deputy got out of the truck slowly, both slamming their doors at the same time. The sheriff was tall and skinny and had a shiny badge pinned to his shirt, just like in the movies. His deputy was smaller and so round in the middle that the material of his shirt strained against the buttons above his belt buckle.

The sheriff pasted a smile on his face and approached her. Robin tried to find his eyes, but he was wearing dark sunglasses and she couldn't see them.

"Your dad around?"

Robin shook her head. She was glad he'd asked her something that didn't require words. She didn't think she could have spoken if she'd wanted to.

"Don't matter," the deputy said to the sheriff. "We can tack these papers to the wall, move this little lady to the side, and get on with our business."

Robin bristled. *Little Lady?*

The sheriff put his hands on his hips and watched as the deputy tacked the papers to the barn a few feet away from her.

The deputy came and stood beside the sheriff, putting his arms on his hips as well. He looked down at Robin and spoke firmly but kindly. "You're breaking the law, you know that, don't you?"

Robin wanted to speak up, wanted to tell them they'd put in their application already, that they would have their certification any day now, but she could barely breathe, let alone speak.

The deputy crossed his arms. His elbows almost jutted into her face. He fired words at her. "We're taking the animals out of here. Step aside."

Robin didn't move. She couldn't move.

The deputy shifted from one foot to another. "You deaf, girl?" He looked at the sheriff then back at Robin. "Step aside!"

Robin still didn't move.

The sheriff's voice wasn't as mean. "Now listen, little girl …"

"It's all right, Chief, I'll just lift her out of the way," the deputy said matter-of-factly. "You're just making it hard on yourself." When Robin said nothing, he shrugged, shoved the cuffs of his shirt up his arms, and came for her.

Robin tensed. She could smell his minty deodorant as he moved his body close. His fleshy hands gripped her waist, then he jerked her up as easily as if he were lifting a small dog. Robin felt her feet come off the ground.

Then the lifting stopped.

"What the —" The deputy put more heft into his lift, tugging harder to pull Robin out of the way, but he couldn't wrench her away. He put her down, and as he did he saw the thick metal bike chain wrapped tightly around her, fastening her to the metal bar that stretched across the barn door.

"Crap!"

The sheriff took off his sunglasses and cleaned the lenses with his shirt sleeve. She could see the glisten of sweat on his forehead. He leaned towards his deputy and whispered. "Smart little squirt!" Then he turned to Robin. "What's your name, kid?"

Robin tried to find her voice, but it was still hiding somewhere. She looked up at his towering presence and squinted. The sun was in her eyes, and she could barely see.

The sheriff slid his long, boney index finger under the bike chain, assessing its weight and thickness.

Robin squirmed. She didn't like the feeling of his fingers so near her body, and with the man so close, she could smell the acrid aroma of coffee on his breath.

"Listen, kid," he said, "you got two choices here. You can undo this and have a perfectly good bike chain at the end of the day, or we'll saw it off, and you'll have a wrecked one. What's it going to be?"

The deputy gave her a mean look. "Either way, we're getting you out of here."

The sheriff took off his hat and ran his hand through his thinning hair. He forced his voice to stay level. "You want to get yourself arrested? Is that what you want?"

When Robin still did not speak, the sheriff snapped at his deputy. "Get the hacksaw."

The deputy brightened. "Yes, sir!"

Robin stood stiffly as she watched the deputy return to the truck. Her eyes began to sting. In seconds, they were going to cut her away and start clearing out the animals. She looked down, willing herself not to cry. Not here. Not now.

Tires sounded on the gravel. Robin's eyes shot up. Zo-Zo! She almost shouted with relief to see her friend speeding up the lane on her bike, her braids flying behind her.

When Zo-Zo saw the sheriff, she jammed on the brakes so hard, her bike spun. She threw it aside and ran to Robin. "I got your message. I —"

"They're taking the animals," Robin cried. She was yelling, but her voice sounded no louder than a hoarse whisper. "As soon as they cut this chain."

Zo-Zo looked down at the bike chain and her hand flew to her mouth. "Cool!" She leaned towards Robin and said in a low tone, "I called some of the other kids...."

The sheriff pushed Zo-Zo aside. "Go on. Get out of here. We have enough problems."

Zo-Zo recovered her balance and walked over to her bike.

The sheriff called back to his deputy. "It's in the box, the one with all the tools —"

As the sheriff shouted instructions, Zo-Zo unwrapped the chain from her handlebars and ran back to Robin, chaining herself in as well.

When the sheriff turned and saw what Zo-Zo had done, he shook his head slowly. He wagged his long finger at them. "If you think you two little girls can stop us, you've got another think coming."

"At least we'll go to jail together," Zo-Zo said quietly to Robin.

The deputy finally found the hacksaw and brought it to the sheriff.

"It would be a lot easier if you just undid your-selves," the sheriff said. "I'll try not to cut you, but —" He eyed his deputy. "Better get the first aid kit."

"He's just trying to scare us," Zo-Zo said, but she closed her eyes as the sheriff began to saw Robin's chain.

Suddenly there was a scream and loud barking. Squirm and Relentless came charging out of the house. Seeing the saw so close to his sister's flesh, Squirm threw himself at the sheriff. Relentless snarled and bared her teeth, ready to attack. The deputy whipped out a bottle from his pocket and sprayed. Relentless yelped with pain and began pawing at her face and eyes.

Robin screamed and tried to run to her dog, but the chain stopped her.

Squirm threw himself at the deputy. "Get away from my dog!"

The deputy grabbed Squirm and held his arms behind his back while the sheriff dragged Relentless to the truck and shoved her inside.

"Stop!" Robin cried. "Stop!" Now her voice *was* loud.

Squirm's face reddened as he screamed. "Leave her alone!" His chest was heaving as he tried to pull in air. When he couldn't, the colour drained from his face. He clutched his chest and fell to the ground.

"He's having an asthma attack!" Frightened now, Robin tried to undo the lock on her bike chain so she could run for the inhaler but couldn't remember the combination. "His inhaler. It's on the fridge." She pointed to the house.

The sheriff rushed off. The screen door banged once, then twice and he was back beside them, inhaler in hand. Kneeling, he pulled Squirm against him. "Here, kid, open your mouth. That's right. Suck it in."

Robin dropped to her knees and took her brother's hand. It felt moist and terribly small. "It's okay, Squirm. It's okay." As the drug in the inhaler took effect, she could feel him relaxing. The wheezing stopped.

"He looks better now," the deputy said.

"You feel better, son?" the sheriff asked. "Sit up a bit." He arranged Squirm on his knee. "My son had asthma. His attacks used to scare the bejesus out of me. But that was before all these new-fangled drugs."

Squirm stood up and eased himself nearer to Robin. The sheriff stood, too, and slapped the earth from his pants. He handed Squirm the inhaler. "Keep this close." He turned to Robin.

"I suggest you take your brother up to the farmhouse now and put him to bed."

Robin knew that the moment she disappeared, the sheriff would take the animals. But what could she do? There was no way she could put her brother at risk, even for the animals. She nodded gravely and took Squirm's hand.

"No!" Squirm yanked away from her grasp.

"You're not well," she said, trying to sound firm. "Let's go up to the house and —"

He reached back, gripped the bike chain, wrapped it around his wrist and held on tight.

The deputy took his hat off as if to let the steam out the top of his head. "This is going from bad to worse." Hearing a sound, he turned and looked down the lane. A bike appeared with another kid on it.

Robin and Zo-Zo cried out at the same time.

"Brodie!"

Robin clapped her hands and grinned.

Behind him rode another boy and a girl from their class. They all stood by their bikes, staring at the scene in front of them.

The sheriff spat. "Get out of here. This is none of your business."

No one moved. The sheriff waved his arms. "Go! Or I'll arrest the lot of you."

Brodie put his bike down and moved to Robin's side. "Go ahead. Arrest me too!"

One by one, the other kids put down their bikes and stood beside Robin.

The sheriff scratched his head. "Well, I'll be —"

The deputy spat. "Fired. And we'll be the laughing-stock of the department when they find out about this!"

The sheriff shrugged. "We're going to need rein-forcements." He trudged back to his truck, calling behind him. "We'll be back. Maybe not today, but we'll be back." His deputy followed, fuming.

When the truck pulled away, the kids cheered and whacked each other on the back. Robin and Zo-Zo gave each other a high five, then she and Brodie did the same.

It wasn't until Robin had unchained herself that she remembered.

"Relentless!"

But the truck was gone. And so was Relentless.

# CHAPTER
# NINETEEN

Robin let her spinning head fall against the back of the wooden deck chair as she watched the flames from the bonfire leap into the darkness. White and gold sparks danced up into the black night as if trying to join the stars overhead. Beside her, Griff sat in the circle wearing a red paper birthday hat. The rest of the family sat around her, their faces glowing from the blaze of the fire.

Robin snuck a look at her dad. Even he looked relaxed tonight. Thank goodness. Was he ever going to talk to her again?

In her lap, Snooze was licking her fingers, and Tugger was trying to chew on her sleeve. Three of the puppies had gone to other families earlier that day and Robin missed them already. But she missed Relentless more. Not having Relentless with her was like not having one of her hands — she was aware of her loss every moment.

At least she still had some puppies to comfort her. What about poor Relentless? She was probably cooped up in some cage somewhere without anyone to pet her. She must be missing her puppies terribly. That thought made Robin's chest ache. Was she ever going to get her dog back?

The booming sound of music thudded across the field from the Kingshots' house. Robin could feel it pulse in the small of her back. She grimaced. All of her class except Zo-Zo would be there, dancing and having a good time at Brittany's birthday party. Was Brodie there? Not if Mr. Kingshot had found out about Brodie chaining himself to the barn. But maybe he hadn't found out. The article in the paper had only given her and her brother's names, referring to the rest as "other young people." They probably had Zo-Zo's dad to thank for that.

For all Robin knew, Brodie might be dancing with Brittany right now. In her mind she saw Brittany wearing something tight and sexy and saw Brodie holding Brittany close.

She wished she could get her brain to stop thinking all these terrible things. But ever since her mother's illness, that just seemed to be what her mind did. Things had become even worse, however, since the sheriff had been there. Now there didn't seem to be a moment when her mind wasn't churning out some worst-case scenario. It was exhausting.

Griff banged her knee against Robin's, and Robin passed her granddaughter a stick, then the bag of marshmallows.

Robin put the puppies back on the leash she had them attached to, shoved a soft, white marshmallow on to the sharp end of the stick and positioned it near the flames.

"You want to toast it, not ignite it," Griff said, edging her stick further from the fire. "Like your brother is about to do."

As if on cue, Squirm's marshmallow burst into a ball of flames.

"Cool!" He blew on it, but so hard that the marshmallow dropped into the fire. "Whoops!"

"Oh, well," Griff said. "The fire deserves some marshmallows too."

Something bright appeared in the darkness, and Robin looked up to see Ari approaching with a cake, its top full of lit candles. Ari had been sucking up to Griff and their dad all day. Robin knew why. She wanted to see Conner and soon. She'd been grounded for leaving Squirm and Robin alone, but since her father had believed Ari's lie about her only having been gone while she made a quick trip to the library, she'd only been grounded for a night.

Squirm started singing "Happy Birthday," and they all joined in. Griff grinned and held her hands to her heart.

"Quick, call the fire department," she said, laughing at the blaze.

"We've had enough government officials here, thank you very much," her son said.

Robin groaned. Uh-oh. Was another lecture on its way? She and her brother had heard several in the last few days.

Griff pulled in a big breath and blew until all the candles went out. She looked tenderly at Ari. "I knew something was up when you wouldn't let me in the kitchen." She cut the cake into brick-sized pieces and passed them around.

Her dad took a big bite. "Scrummy." He smiled at Ari. His eyes moved to Robin, and his smile disappeared. He hadn't smiled at her since he'd found out about the sheriff. They'd had to tell him. And when they did, he'd looked at her and Squirm as if they were teasing. He had been deeply shocked to find out they weren't.

"You locked yourself to the barn with *bike chains*?"

"We stopped them, Dad," Squirm had said, his voice swollen with pride.

Griff had suppressed a smile.

Her father's voice landed hard, like a gavel. "You could have been hurt."

*How*? Robin had wanted to ask, but if there was one thing she'd learned, it was not to ask questions when her father was angry.

She and Squirm then got lecture #1, which was about laws being there for a reason, which led to lecture #2, about having respect for those laws even if you didn't agree with them.

"But what if a law isn't right?" Robin had asked Griff.

Her father jumped in. "If a law isn't right, you work to change it. Through proper channels."

Griff looked at him questioningly. "Aren't we already doing that? We've had our wildlife application in for a while now."

Her father sighed. "I guess a wildlife license is like a driver's license. You either have one or you don't. There's no in-betweens."

Robin felt a question press up into her throat. "Dad — would you have let the sheriff take the animals?" She couldn't believe he would have. Not if that risked them being put to sleep.

Her father said nothing.

"I don't think your dad knows what he would have done," Griff said. "I guess we'll have to wait until the sheriff comes back to find out."

Squirm snapped to attention. "Will he come back?"

"Of course he will," Griff said. "You can bet your bottom dollar."

Robin cringed. That scared her, but there was something that scared her even more. "What about Relentless? Are we going to get her back?" Even saying her dog's name made her chest tighten.

Griff frowned. "You can bet the sheriff isn't going to make getting her back easy — he's probably being kidded blue in the face down at the station for being outsmarted by a couple of kids. I wouldn't put it past him to make us wait awhile."

Robin's heart lurched. "But they can't keep her, can they?"

Griff shook her head. "No, but they'll take their sweet time returning her. Just to make sure we understand who's running the show."

That talk had been well over a week ago now, and Relentless still wasn't back. Griff had phoned the authorities every day but hadn't been able to find out anything. She told Robin repeatedly that there was nothing to worry about, that they would get Relentless back, that it was just a matter of time, but Robin worried anyway.

What if they forgot to feed Relentless? What if her dog got sick? Even died? Robin yanked her mind away from this last thought as if she might pull herself back from the edge of a fifty storey building.

Now, at the party, Robin ate her cake and watched as Griff clicked on a small camper's headlight and picked up the paper. She went straight to the editorial page.

"Two more letters to the editor." She scanned them quickly. "Both *supporting* us! That's good news. Now let's see what's happening with the campaign." She flipped some pages and continued reading. A huge smile blossomed on her face. "Ed Goodings has publicly come out in favour of the animal shelter! Says here that if he's elected, he'll even fund it." She patted Robin's leg hard. "What a great birthday present that is." She returned to the article. "He even gives some stats about the number of animals we've helped."

"Stats you probably fed him," her son said.

"Of course!" Griff reached for a large chunk of cake and ate it quickly. "We're finally on the political map." She licked her lips. "Get us animal lovers stirred up, and look out."

They all sat quietly for a while, then their father spoke. "I ran into Tom at the hardware store today. He said the sheriff's been organizing reinforcements from other towns." His hand moved up to the cell phone he was now keeping, fully charged and switched on, in his front pocket.

"Sounds like he's going to come with an army," Griff said, sucking icing sugar from the tips of her fingers. "We better prepare for battle."

Her son lurched himself straight up in his chair. "There will be no battle here." He eyed Robin and Squirm. "I have your word, right?"

Squirm nodded dolefully. Robin did as well. Was it lying if you broke a promise you didn't say out loud?

They all stared into the fire. The silence was broken by the sound of car doors slamming.

Their dad's head jolted up. He and Griff exchanged alarmed glances. Robin felt herself tense. Would the sheriff come this late at night?

Ari jumped up. "Conner —"

Conner appeared with two other friends.

"What a surprise," Ari said, moving towards them.

"But you said to —" Conner stopped. "Oh, yeah, well, um, we were just going by and we saw the fire and …"

"Well, Conner, you won't get an Emmy for that bit of acting, but here, have some cake anyway!" Griff held the platter of cake towards him and his friends.

"I made it," Ari said proudly. She introduced everyone then took her friends down to the dock. Soon there were shrieks and splashing sounds.

Griff shivered. "Isn't it a little early in the season for swimming?"

Squirm nudged Robin. "I want to go swimming too. Let's go."

Robin shook her head.

Squirm's smile collapsed.

"You go anyway, Squirm," his dad said. "Just don't let yourself get too cold."

Squirm leapt up and ran off.

Robin sank down in her chair. She didn't want to swim with Ari and her friends, but soon her own friends would be asking her to go. What was she going to do then?

"Don't be too hard on yourself," Griff said, cutting another small piece of cake. "I've had lots of fears in my life, but I got over them. You will too."

Robin looked at her doubtfully.

Griff handed her a small bag. "Maybe this will help."

Robin looked at her with confusion. "But this is *your* birthday. *You're* the one who's supposed to get presents."

"I know, but I've had this for a while. I've just been waiting for the right time to give it to you."

Robin pulled the drawstring apart and pulled out a silver pendant of a dog. A dog that looked just like Relentless. A well of yearning flooded into her throat.

"Remember our talk about totems?" Griff asked.

"Those animal spirit things? The ones that protect you?" Robin ran her fingers along the glossy surface of the charm. She liked how solid it felt. And warm.

Griff smiled. "I got you this so you'd remember that you have help. It's not just you against your fear of water. It's you and me and your dad and brother and Relentless, when she comes back. And this wonderful totem, this dog spirit. All together we're *way* bigger than your fear. You'll see. You *will* learn to swim again. And it won't be anywhere near as scary as you think."

Robin wanted to believe that, wished she could, but somehow she didn't.

When Squirm appeared, shaking with cold from his swim, Griff wrapped a beach towel around him and pulled him onto her lap.

Car lights flashed again.

"Grand central station," Griff said.

Again, Robin felt herself stiffen.

A large man approached. He was carrying a flashlight, so Robin couldn't see who it was, but the man's height reminded her of the sheriff. She gripped the paddle-shaped arms of her chair.

Her father stood and they all stared as the man came towards them. A smaller person ran out in front of the man.

Zo-Zo appeared and stopped at the edge of their circle, bouncing on her toes excitedly. Brodie appeared beside her. He looked just as excited.

Robin stared at them. What was going on? Why were they all here?

Griff touched Mr. Donnelly's arm. "Hello, Peter. Join us for some cake."

Zo-Zo grabbed Robin's hand and pulled it to her chest. "Guess what? Guess!"

Brodie grinned. "We're going to be on TV!"

Peter smiled broadly. "A company named The Energy Alliance got word of the kid's eco-contest and wants to use it in schools across the country."

"The Big Fat Footprint?" Robin felt giddy. Was it really true?

"They're offering a chunk of change for the honour too," Zo-Zo's dad added.

Robin, Brodie, and Zo-Zo threw themselves into a huddle of a hug. Robin's dad pulled up some extra chairs and added some logs to the fire while Griff handed out pieces of cake.

After they'd all eaten and discussed every detail of The Energy Alliance deal, Zo-Zo picked up one of the puppies and turned to Robin, then Brodie. "Hey, I think we should have a sleepover. To celebrate."

"What a good idea," Griff said. "You can all sleep in the loft of the barn."

Robin looked at her dad. "Can we, Dad? Please?" She could see her father debating. "You let Ari have Conner visit."

Her father gave her a sharp look.

"Conner?" Pete Donnelly asked. "Conner Kingshot?"

"You know him?" Griff asked.

"My dad knows everyone," Zo-Zo said.

Mr. Donnelly pulled Zo-Zo's braid affectionately. "Did a story on the bush party he organized last year. Around about this time, too. Had about three hundred kids and a fire that took out about twenty trees. Good thing there wasn't a wind, or it would have been worse."

"I heard about it," Griff said.

"Was Conner charged?" Robin's dad asked.

"Rick *Kingshot's* son, charged?" Mr. Donnelly shrugged. "Not likely."

Robin's dad stared into the fire.

Robin pulled him from his reverie. "So, can they stay, Dad? Can they?"

"I don't see why not," he said. "As long as Brodie calls his mom."

The three kids ran up to the house. Zo-Zo and Robin collected sleeping bags while Brodie called home. When they had his mom's agreement, they took the bags out to the barn and carried them up the steps to the loft. Robin could still hear the music from the party next door, but now it didn't bother her at all.

# CHAPTER TWENTY

Brodie was visiting with Mukwa while Robin and Zo-Zo unwrapped binder twine from two hay bales and began distributing the hay to make soft under-padding for their sleeping bags.

"He sure likes that bear cub," Zo-Zo said as she unrolled her sleeping bag.

When Brodie came up the ladder, he brought Snooze with him. "I couldn't resist," he said, nuzzling the puppy.

Zo-Zo turned to him. "So, how come you're not at Brittany's?"

Brodie shrugged. "At Brittany's? I didn't want to go. Besides, I didn't think I'd be welcome anyway. Not after Rick fired me."

Zo-Zo's eyes looked huge through the thick lenses of her glasses. "He fired you?"

Brodie pressed his lips together and nodded. "Now he wants the bike back."

"That's not fair!" Robin said.

"Told you he was a creep," Zo-Zo said.

Brodie let out a long breath. "He was nice to me for a while."

"Yeah, as long as you were friends with Brittany," Zo-Zo said.

Brodie shrugged. "I'm in his bad books now. *Both* their bad books."

"Join the club," Robin said, smiling shyly.

Zo-Zo threw some hay into the air. "None of that matters now. We're going to be on national TV!" She grinned. "I still can't believe they're paying us!"

"Hey!" Brodie said, flicking off the hay that was landing on his head. Zo-Zo tossed some hay right at him, and he lunged at her. Zo-Zo laughed and rolled away, but Brodie was unable to stop his momentum and fell into Robin.

Robin fell back, and their faces were so close she could smell his skin. He smiled at her, and Robin felt herself blush. They both pulled away at the same time.

"Okay, you two — don't make me feel like a third wheel!" Zo-Zo wiggled down into her bag. "What should we do with the money? Use it to buy food for the animals?"

Robin sighed. "If the animals are still here. Dad found out the sheriff is getting a whole bunch of 'reinforcements' from other towns."

"Good thing we've got our own 'reinforcements,'" Zo-Zo said.

Brodie's eyebrows shot up. "What does *that* mean?"

"The kids on my blog," Zo-Zo said. "There's over thirty! And they've all promised to fight if the sheriff shows up —"

"Sounds like all-out war!" Brodie said. He looked at Robin with concern.

In the dim light, Zo-Zo's eyes were big. "I can't wait to see the look on the sheriff's face when he sees us all."

Brodie moved his eyes back to Zo-Zo. "What are you going to do? Chain everyone in again?"

"This time, we're going to fight back, that's what we're going to do." Zo-Zo said, her face resolute and intense.

Shivers ricocheted down Robin back. She wiggled further down into her bag.

"Fight all you want, but it won't do you any good," Brodie said. "Not if Mr. Kingshot wins the election. He can be ruthless."

"So can we," Zo-Zo said. "Just watch."

Brodie grimaced. "You're scaring me, Zo-Zo."

"What choice do we have?" Zo-Zo retorted. "Are you going to let him kill Mukwa? Your favourite bear?"

Brodie looked deeply disturbed. "Mr. Kingshot told me once that the only good bear was a dead bear! He was only half-joking, but —"

"Sounds like Conner," Robin said. "He calls Mukwa his 'bear rug.'"

"Like father like son." Zo-Zo scrunched up her face. "Your sister's going out with Conner, right?"

Robin nodded. "Usually, she's got boys wrapped around her little finger, but not this time."

"Is your dad letting her go to that bush party?" Zo-Zo asked.

Brodie's eyebrows shot up. "Your dad would *let* her? Those things are drunken brawls."

Robin sighed. "She's going to sneak out."

"Whoa," Brodie said.

"Do you think I should tell my dad?" Robin asked.

Zo-Zo bit her lip. "No. You can't. Kids' code."

Brodie shrugged but didn't argue. "It's this weekend. Conner and his dad were talking about it in the office before I got fired. Mr. Kingshot's getting him some beer."

"For a dad, he sure doesn't act like one," Zo-Zo said. She pulled the corner of her mouth into her cheek. "What I don't get is why he's so against this place? I mean, what's a few hurt animals to a guy like him?"

"He wants the property," Brodie said. "For a hog farm. I saw the plans he's drawn up at his office. There's a lot of money in hogs."

Zo-Zo laughed. "Hogs! He's such a hog himself."

"I sure hope Ed Goodings gets elected," Robin said.

Zo-Zo shook her head. "Fat chance of that! Kingshot *will* get elected, and when he does, he's going to come here with an army of cops. We've got to be prepared. I've been collecting stones and making slingshots and —"

Brodie interrupted. "Stones? Slingshots? Those things can hurt people."

Robin put her hands over her ears. "Enough." She was getting really frightened.

Brodie and Zo-Zo settled into their sleeping bags, and Robin bunched up her sweater to use it as a pillow. She turned off her headlamp and the others did too.

Lying in the darkness, Robin felt agitated. Her mind kept producing images of Zo-Zo throwing stones as dozens of policemen charged towards her, billy clubs raised. To calm herself, she took some long deep breaths.

Beneath her she could hear the sounds of the animals below. They were muted sounds at this time of night, but still, she could hear rustling, snuffling, scratching, some soft mewing, quacking, and grunting. The sounds comforted her. She yawned and felt herself slipping down into the arms of sleep.

She awoke abruptly, feeling breathless. She'd been having her drowning dream again. Pushing herself up, she threw off the sleeping bag until she stopped feeling so sweaty. When she could breathe normally again, she made her way to the ladder that went down to the main part of the barn. She had to pee.

She had her headlight with her, but with the moon shining through the slats in the barn, she could see easily. The wooden rungs of the ladder were smooth against the bare skin of her feet as she made her way down them. Outside the barn, the ground was moist from the dew. She looked up. The night sky was sprinkled with the glitter of a million stars. Stunned by the huge magnificence of it, she stood still for several minutes and just stared. Then she walked a few feet from the barn and squatted in a patch of grass. As she peed, there was a sound. A strange, guttural sound. On high alert, she forced herself to be absolutely still. And listened acutely.

Then she heard it again. A half grunt, half growl, but big and breathy somehow like a sound that would come from a big-chested animal. A long-nailed paw of fear clawed through her. She squinted into the darkness.

She couldn't see it, but she could smell it now, the strong animal musk.

Then it stood up on its hind legs.

Robin's eyes followed it to its full height. Her breath caught in her throat.

The mother bear!

Maybe it was because Robin was used to Mukwa, who was still so small. Or, maybe it was because of the way the moon was casting shadows, but the mother looked absolutely colossal.

Robin gulped. Slowly, very slowly, she stood, easing her pajama bottoms up as she did. The bear was watching her. Getting ready to pounce! In one, or maybe two quick strides, the bear would be on her, ripping her skin with its claws and breaking her bones with its powerful teeth. Should she run? Should she lie down and pretend to be dead? She couldn't remember what she was supposed to do. Her brain was mushy. Her legs felt like they were going to collapse.

There was another sound, a different sound. It took Robin a moment to figure out what it was. Keeping her eyes on the bear, she was aware at the periphery of her vision that through the wide open barn door, someone was bounding down the ladder.

The bear heard the sound too. It huffed, moving from one foot to another as it prepared to charge. Robin could feel its agitation.

Suddenly the footsteps stopped.

"Whoa!"

Brodie spoke only the one word, but it was soaked with fascinated fear.

Would the bear come for her or Brodie first? She was closer, but Brodie was nearer to Mukwa. In either case, the mother bear was close enough to kill either of them with a swipe of her meaty arm. Robin tried to swallow, but her throat was too dry. She opened her mouth but no words came out. What would she say anyway?

Mukwa stirred in the barn and made urgent grunts. Then Robin remembered. What she remembered allowed her to speak.

"Your baby, you want your baby —"

Getting these words out took huge effort. She took a small breath. "I'll get him, I'll —"

Robin inched towards the barn and Mukwa's enclosure, hoping the mother bear would somehow realize she wasn't going to hurt her baby, but let him loose. It took forever to get there. Once she was inside, her fingers fumbled with the latch on Mukwa's cage. She couldn't get it to open. She felt a sudden motion and shut her eyes, waiting for the devastation of the mother bear's claws. But it wasn't the mother bear. It was Brodie, helping her with the latch. There was a clicking sound. The cage door swung open.

Mukwa bolted past her and out the barn door. His waiting mother went down on all fours in exuberant greeting. She sniffed then turned quickly and led her baby away from the barn.

Robin watched them disappear into the safety of the dark woods. She threw her arm across her chest and let out a big sigh of relief.

Brodie leaned towards her. "You all right?"

Robin fell against him, and for a brief moment, they held each other up. She could hear her heart pounding. And feel Brodie's too, as if in answer.

# CHAPTER TWENTY-ONE

Everyone was glad that Mukwa was now back with his mother.

"I didn't really have to take his cast off," her dad had commented. "It will disintegrate on its own anyway."

As happy as Robin was that Mukwa and his mother were reunited, she missed the baby bear. Mukwa's return to the wild seemed to make Relentless's absence all the more unbearable. And, as if these two things weren't difficult enough, she had this terrible dilemma about whether to spill the beans about her sister going to the bush party.

Robin felt as if her insides were in a tug of war. One part of her was vehement that she should tell her dad about Ari's plan to sneak out. Another part argued just as strongly that she should say nothing. At the moment, the part that thought she should stay out of it was winning. So she made up her mind. She would keep her mouth shut. But as soon as she'd made this decision, she had the awful thought that something bad might happen at the bush party, and she was thrown into the gruesome debate once again.

The day of the bush party, she wandered downstairs in her pajamas and stepped out on the porch. Her dad was doing the barn chores that morning, and she was glad for the break. She sat down on the steps and felt the sun wrap itself around her like a hug. The lake was spread out before her, so still, as if it hadn't woken up yet either.

She looked around for Relentless. She did this dozens of times every day, forgetting. Soon she'd go down to the barn and get some of the puppies. They only had a few left now: Greedy Guts, Einstein, Snooze, and Tugger. She was glad Snooze and Einstein were still with them, since she wanted those two puppies to go to Brodie and Squirm. Both Zo-Zo's dad and Brodie's mom, however, had yet to agree to the adoption.

Looking out over the lake, she saw a red canoe in the distance. She watched it for a while and realized it was Griff paddling back from Berry Island. Her stroke was long and smooth, and the boat cut through the calm water like an arrow. Robin reached up and touched her necklace. She liked the feel of it, although she had to admit, it had done little to lessen her fear of water. Maybe this totem stuff was just a bunch of bunk. Robin went down to the dock, the dew-wet grasses licking the bare skin on her feet and legs. She arrived in time to catch the front of the canoe as Griff paddled in.

"Thought I'd get some quiet time," Griff said. "Before the traffic starts!" She tied up the boat, set her thermos of tea on the dock and pulled off her life-jacket. She hoisted herself into one of the two big green Muskoka chairs.

"I used to take my quiet time with Mukwa in the mornings, but now, thanks to you, she's back in the wild with her mom. In fact, I thought I saw the two of them over on the far side of Berry Island." Griff leaned back in the chair. "Where are Squirm and Ari?"

"Squirm's at his friend's. Ari's upstairs writing in her diary."

Reminded of her dilemma, Robin started chewing her thumbnail.

Griff poured some tea from the thermos into the little plastic cup that doubled as a cap. "Here — have some of this. It'll taste better than your fingernail."

Robin took a sip. The tea was hot and tasted of lemon and honey. She liked it. "Can I ask you something?"

"'Course."

Robin debated how to phrase her question.

"Just spit it out," Griff said.

"Well, what if you knew someone was going to do something they shouldn't — not like something really bad, but something that *maybe* could get them into trouble. Would you tell?"

"You're talking about the bush party, right? Is Ari going to try and sneak out?"

Robin's jaw dropped. How could Griff know?

"I was a teenager once, too, you know," Griff said. "I snuck out a time or two." A warm smile erupted on her face. Then she brought her eyes back to Robin's. "Anyways, I'm not surprised Ari's thinking about sneaking out. She's desperate to go and your dad won't let her. What self-respecting teenager wouldn't be thinking of sneaking out? But *thinking* about it is one thing, actually doing it is another."

"You going to stop her?"

Griff raised her hands into the air and made "stop" signs of her palms. "How? Put bars on the windows?" Her hands collapsed back to her lap. "Ari is getting to the age where she's going to have to make her own choices. She's not a little girl any more." She gazed at Robin. "And neither are you. By the way, that was very mature the way you faced the mother bear the other night. Very brave."

Brave? Robin shrugged. She hadn't felt brave. She'd felt terrified.

Griff poured more tea. "Remember what I said? Courage isn't about *not* having fear. It's about having fear and doing something anyway."

Robin was considering this when Griff spoke again. "You did the exact right thing, letting Mukwa go."

"Brodie let him out of the cage, not me."

"He told me he just helped you," Griff said. She blew on her tea. "By the way, I like that boy. He obviously thinks you're pretty special too."

Robin searched Griff's eyes. Did he?

"I don't say things I don't mean," Griff said.

Robin blushed. When it came to Brodie, she felt so uncertain. Sure, he was hanging around the animal shelter a lot lately, but that was because of the bear, wasn't it? Besides, at the moment, both Brittany and her father were mad at him. That would change, wouldn't it? What would happen then?

Robin put her head in her hands. As usual, her thoughts were driving her crazy! They swarmed around her like insects. If it wasn't worries about Brodie, it was worries about Relentless. Or the sheriff. What were they going to do when he came back? Should she stay inside the house as she had promised her father or call Zo-Zo and her gang of kids for a big battle? There were so many things she had to decide, but she had no idea *how* to decide.

She collapsed down onto the edge of Griff's chair.

Griff refilled the small thermos cup again and passed it to Robin. "Well, all I can say is that it must be wonderful for Mukwa to be back with his mother. I bet he'd just about given up hope of ever seeing her again. Every kid needs their mother."

A wave of despair washed into Robin's chest and throat. She tensed and tried to push the feelings down, but they wouldn't go. With a little more time, she would have been able to gather the energy required to hold them off, but Griff reached forward and pulled Robin gently back so she was leaning against her. The warmth of Griff's body shocked her. Robin hadn't been this close to someone since —

She yanked herself forward, but Griff eased her close once again. Weakened by the comfort, Robin let herself fall against her grandmother. Tears started to drip down her face. Then, before she could stop them, sounds erupted from her mouth, awful, sobbing sounds.

"It's all right," Griff whispered. "It's all right." She stroked Robin's shoulders. "Just let it go, my sweet girl. Let it all go."

Robin couldn't have stopped the emotions now if she'd tried. They were too strong, and she felt too frail.

She cried and cried while Griff held her. She hated crying like this, but in a way, it was a relief to let go.

Griff rubbed her back. "That's right, cry those tears right out of you. Till there's no more left."

After a few more minutes, she pulled out a hankie and wiped Robin's face. Out on the lake, a loon called. Another answered.

They both listened for a long moment. "I don't know what it is about wilderness," Griff said. "Maybe it's just so big that it makes everything else seem small, but it settles me somehow. Gets me feeling really quiet. That's when *I* feel your mom. It's like she's right here. Or her spirit is — in the wind and the water and the call of the loons."

Robin liked that thought, but it made her want to cry again.

Griff poured the last of the tea into the tiny cup. "It's all such a mystery. A mystery so big I can't really understand it, but so wonderful I don't even want to try."

Robin reached for the cup at the same time as her grandmother and the two of them jostled for it. Griff laughed then Robin laughed, and the tea spilled a bit, and they both laughed more.

Robin was shooting back the last of the tea when she heard the farmhouse door *fwap*. Her father called down to Griff.

"Be up in a minute!" Griff called then turned to Robin. "I'm going to do some canvassing for Ed Goodings this morning. I keep telling all the animal lovers, a vote for Ed is a vote for The Wild Place."

Robin shrugged. "Brittany's telling everyone her father's victory is a done deal. She says he's hardly even campaigning, he's so sure."

Griff made a hooting sound. "Good. It's just that kind of arrogance that might bring him down." She stood up.

"Brodie says Kingshot wants to put a hog farm on this property."

"Wouldn't that just be the ticket! That should make him feel right at home!"

Robin looked at Griff. "If he gets elected, will he be able to take this place away?"

"Over my dead body."

Robin frowned. She didn't want to think about her gran as a dead body.

"Mom!" Robin's dad called down to the dock. "Come on. I've got a rescue to do on the way back. Let's go."

"Music to my ears," Griff said, gathering her things. "Music to my ears." She planted a warm kiss on Robin's forehead and made her way up the steps.

# CHAPTER
# TWENTY-TWO

That night, Ari announced she wasn't feeling well and was going to bed early.

Their father rushed around getting her Aspirin and making her a hot drink. When he gave it to her, he felt her forehead. "You're not hot," he said.

*She's not hot because she's not sick!* Robin wanted to scream. *She's going to bed early so she can get up in the middle of the night and sneak out!*

Robin glared at her sister and was surprised to see how flushed Ari's face was. Her eyes looked glassy too. Could she actually *be* sick? Robin doubted it, but in a way, she hoped her sister was. If she was too sick to sneak out to the bush party, Robin wouldn't have to worry.

Robin went upstairs about an hour after Ari and found her sister in bed, her eyes closed. Was she asleep or just pretending? At the bottom of the bed, on a stool, was a pile of clothes: jeans, a thick jacket, warm socks.

The words were out before she could stop herself. "Those look like bush party clothes to me."

Ari turned quickly. Her eyes were huge. And pleading. "Don't tell. Please."

Robin couldn't remember the last time her sister had asked her to do anything, let alone said the word "please." She looked away and got into her pajamas. When she turned out the light, she whispered. "Be careful, okay? Just be careful."

The next thing she knew, something red was swirling around the room. It was a light, a bright neon light. She was at a carnival, on the Ferris wheel and —

She opened her eyes, pulling herself from the dream. She wasn't at a carnival at all, but at home. In her room. What confused her was the fact that the red light was still there, circling the ceiling. It was weird. She lay there for a moment, feeling totally disoriented. Then she heard voices, men's voices, and realized that the red light was flashing through the window from outside. She jerked her head around. Ari was there, in her bed. Or was she? Robin leaned forward and pushed her fingers gently into the heap of blankets. The pile was nothing but pillows!

She sat up. The clock on the bureau said five a.m. She peeled away the covers and crawled over to the window. There, parked in her driveway, was a police car with a flashing red light.

Robin whirled around and tip-toed along the hallway until she could hear what was going on downstairs.

"Thank you for bringing her home, officer," Griff said. Her voice sounded flat and very tired.

"She was passed out when I found her," an unfamiliar male voice said. "I couldn't rouse her at first, and

I was worried about alcohol poisoning, so I thought I'd better find her parents."

"We appreciate that," her father said gravely.

Robin could hear retching sounds coming from the downstairs toilet, followed by low, agonized groaning.

"She won't feel like drinking again for a while, I'm sure," the officer said. There was the sound of a chair scraping across the floor. "I'd best be on my way. Now all I have to do is deal with the other hundred and fifty drunken kids out there."

"Is that how many were at the party?" Griff asked.

"I'm guessing," he answered. "Most of them scattered when we showed up. The ones that could still move."

"Any sign of a boy named Conner?" Robin heard her father ask.

"Conner? The organizer? Yeah, we pulled him away from some lipstick-smeared redhead. He wasn't too coherent either. One of the other officers is taking the girl home."

There were scraping sounds as more chairs were pushed away from the table. Robin stumbled quickly back to bed. In a few moments, she heard her father coming upstairs.

"Steady. That's it. Three more and you're there."

When they came into the bedroom, Robin kept her eyes shut. She didn't want either of them to know she was awake. Through squinted eyes, she watched as her father eased Ari into bed. Gently he tucked the covers over her and stood near, pushing his fingers through his hair, and staring at her. Hurriedly, he planted a kiss on her forehead and left.

Robin listened to her sister whimpering and groaning in her sleep for the rest of the night.

In the morning, Robin put on her robe and went into the kitchen. No one was there. She wandered down to Griff's.

"What happened to Ari?"

Griff yawned tiredly. "Why are you asking me? I saw you peeking from the top of the stairs."

Robin shrugged. There was no point in denying it. "Sounds like she got completely wasted. I can hardly believe it."

"Wasted. That's the exact right word. Wasted." Griff shook her head. "Which, I'm guessing, is probably what Conner wanted."

"Huh?"

"I'm not saying that to let Ari off the hook. Bottom line, it's still her responsibility to stay sober. Or at least coherent. But I'm guessing Conner really loaded up her drinks with alcohol." She rubbed her open palms up and down her thighs. "Problem was, sounds like Ari passed out and spoiled his fun. So he dumped her and headed off with another girl."

Robin felt sick. Her poor sister.

"Your dad's pretty upset, but I'm looking on the bright side."

Robin stared at Griff. What bright side?

"Hopefully, when Ari finds out what kind of guy Conner really is, she'll drop him. Not that I'm going to say that to her. I want her to reach that conclusion herself."

Griff gathered her things. "Anyways, I'm heading into town to do some more canvassing for Ed Goodings. With the election so close, we've got to pour on the pressure." She headed towards the door. "You be kind to Ari today, okay? She's really suffering. But keep your distance. My guess is she's going to be prickly as a porcupine."

It wasn't hard to keep her distance from Ari, because her sister stayed in bed all that day. She didn't get up for dinner either. The day after that was a school day, but when the alarm went off, Ari did not rouse herself. A few minutes later, her father came into the bedroom and shook her.

"Ari get up. It's a school day."

Ari groaned. When she spoke, her voice was whining and weak. "Dad, I can't go. I'm sick, I —"

Her father cleared his throat. "Ari, you're not staying home because you're still getting over a hangover!"

Ari started to plead. "But school's almost over, it doesn't matter, we —"

"You're going!"

Ari yanked on some jeans and an old T-shirt. Without even putting on her make-up, she stomped down the stairs and sat at the kitchen table, her arms folded, her red and watery eyes to the floor.

Griff put her hand on Ari's shoulder, but she pulled away.

For days, Ari didn't speak. When she wasn't in school, she stayed in her room, only coming out for meals, something their father insisted she do. At the table, she didn't speak and no one spoke to her. Even Squirm stayed out of her way.

On the weekend, when the local paper came out, the headline on the front page read BUSH PARTY BUST! Below the headline was a photo of a gang of kids by a huge fire. Standing at the centre was Conner with his arm around a red-headed girl who looked as if she was about to fall over.

Griff sighed and set the paper in the middle of the breakfast table. "Well, if this doesn't wake Ari up, nothing will."

"What do you mean?"

"You'll see," she said, standing up. "What are you up to today?"

"Zo-Zo is coming over later," Robin said. "We're going to clean out some cages. Brodie might come too."

"Squirm's at Tom's?"

"Yup."

"If that boy Josh comes to see the baby owl today, see if you can get Ari to come out and see him, okay? I think he likes her. Don't you?"

Robin rolled her eyes. All boys liked Ari.

"She just might need some cheering up," Griff said.

Robin nodded. "I've never seen her this way. She's like, depressed. She doesn't even answer the phone." Ari wasn't eating either. Her sister's already model-thin body was turning stick-thin. And she had dark bags under her eyes. She looked terrible. But what was even scarier was that Ari didn't care.

"Oh, well," Griff sighed. "She'll come around. Just like your father did."

Suddenly she clapped her hands together. "Oh, guess what?" She grinned. "I think I know where they're keeping Relentless!" Her eyes flashed. "Your dad and I are going to go there after we do some canvassing and see if we can bust her out. If they won't listen to your dad, maybe they'll listen to a frail, little old lady like me." She winked at Robin and went off.

When Griff and her dad had gone, Robin got herself a bowl of cereal. Since no one was around, she added a handful of chocolate chips and took the comic section of the newspaper out to the porch. She couldn't stop thinking about Relentless. Would Griff and her dad be able to bring the dog home? Excitement bubbled through her body. "Please, please, please, please," she whispered.

When she was done reading the comics, she went inside to get more cereal. The newspaper with the headline about the bush party was shredded into a pile of ripped up bits of paper. Ari's work, obviously.

Robin listened quietly for a few moments. Had Ari gone back to their room? Or was she on her way to Conner's place to beat him up? Robin looked out the window to make sure Ari wasn't tromping across the field to the Kingshots', but there was no sign of her.

Strange as it felt, Robin was sad for Ari. As Griff said, her sister was suffering and Robin couldn't help but feel bad for her. So bad that she went upstairs to look for her. Ari was not in their bedroom. Robin spent a few minutes cleaning up her side of the room. She even unpacked the last of her boxes. Maybe that would make Ari feel better.

When she was done, she stood back and surveyed the room. For the first time ever, her side looked cleaner than Ari's. But that wasn't saying much, because Ari's side was strewn with discarded clothes, old shoes, and scattered magazines. Even her make-up case, which was usually kept in pristine condition, sat overturned, its guts spilling out over the floor.

Robin went back downstairs, poured more cereal into her bowl, added more chocolate chips and went back outside. Listlessly, she picked the chocolate chips out of her cereal. She felt nervous, like something bad was going to happen. Her stomach felt wobbly and tense all at the same time. Was Griff going to come back and tell her Relentless was dead? Wanting some distraction, she picked up the binoculars on the table and scanned the lake. It was weird the way the binoculars made things so big and close. Using them made her feel like Super Girl with X-ray eyes.

She scrutinized the cottages down in the bay then scanned the shore all the way along to Berry Island. Even though the island was a distance away, in the binoculars it looked close enough to touch. She searched it from one end to the other and was just about to put the binoculars aside when she saw two bears lumbering along the far shore, behind Berry Island. Robin stood. It was Mukwa! Mukwa and her mom!

Robin stood up, happiness surging through her as she watched them slip into the water and begin swimming towards the island. Robin smiled. Once upon a time, she'd been able to swim effortlessly like that. But that was before. Before she'd almost drowned. Before her mother. Before fear had gotten into her body and immobilized her. That was the crazy thing. She *knew* how to swim. Fear just made it impossible to do it.

She turned her attention back to the bears. They were moving steadily across the large expanse of water. The bears were about halfway to the island when there was a loud, machine-like roar.

Robin's body went rigid. She knew what that sound meant.

Two Jet Skis zoomed out on to the lake. They were black with yellow flames licking along the sides.

At first, Robin thought maybe Conner and Brittany hadn't seen the bears. She waited for them to catch sight of them then veer away. But they didn't. In fact, the bears seemed to be the bullseye they were targeting.

Robin ran down to the dock, shouting as loud as she could. "Leave them! Leave them alone!"

There was no way they could hear her. Not that they would listen anyway.

She paced furiously, moving the binoculars back and forth between the bears and the boats. As the boats sped closer, the bears sensed the danger and turned, swimming back the way they'd come. But the Jet Skis were closing in.

When Conner was close to Mukwa, he cut the forward motion of the Jet Ski and stood. Robin watched with horror as he swirled a long rope over his head like a cowboy. When he had the lasso spinning, he propelled it through the air. On the third try, he made it land around Mukwa's neck. Conner put the Jet Ski in forward. The rope tightened, jolting Mukwa forward. Slowly, Conner began dragging his captive behind him.

Mukwa went under. Robin gasped. She wanted to jump in the canoe and paddle over, but her body was frozen with fear, making it impossible to move.

Helplessly, she watched Mukwa struggling, splashing to get away, but he couldn't. He was no match for Conner and the power of his Jet Ski.

A hot wave of outrage flooded over her, and she forced herself into the canoe. It was tippy and lurched as she got into it. She grabbed the sides and held on, fear immobilizing her once again. She *hated* her fear, *hated* it more than anything ever.

A paddle clattered to the floor of the canoe just in front of her knees. Robin looked up as Ari tossed two life jackets into the boat and scrambled in behind her, paddle in hand.

"Come on. Let's get there before he kills them."

With a hefty shove, Ari pushed them away from the dock.

Robin's hands were shaking so hard she had difficulty picking up the paddle. Behind her, Ari began paddling hard, giving it all her strength. Robin forced her arms to move. Seeing the bears up ahead filled her with resolve. She plunged her paddle deep into the water. The boat sped forward. She was still afraid, still terrified, but she paddled anyway.

For a moment, she thought she could hear her father shouting from the shore, but she couldn't stop to look, even for a second.

"Stroke! Stroke! Stroke!" Ari called from behind.

When they reached the Jet Skis, Ari tried to steer the canoe between Conner and Mukwa. It took her a few minutes to get herself in position and when she was, she grabbed the rope. Conner yanked on it, trying to get her to release it, but Ari held on. As they struggled, Brittany manoeuvred her boat near and was reaching to the side to get the rope herself so she could pull it out of Ari's hands when Conner gunned his engine. His Jet Ski lurched forward, leaving a huge wave swelling behind it. The wave slammed against Brittany's Jet Ski and threw her off balance. To stabilize herself, she reached for the canoe.

That's when Robin's worst nightmare came true. The canoe flipped over, tossing both her and her sister into the lake.

The cold water grabbed her, sucking her down into its depths. The weight of her body made that easy. She flailed her arms and tried to kick her way to the surface, but fear immobilized her, stiffening her arms and legs so they would barely move. Then she swallowed some water. A terrible, desperate fear filled her. She was going to drown.

Over her head, she could see the surface. It was light-filled and shimmery. Her lungs screamed for it, her muscles screamed for it, every fiber of her life force screamed for it, but it was too far away. She was going to die. Right here, right now. More water came into her mouth.

Something appeared in front of her. Something dark. The mass of it was coming towards her. With her last ounce of energy, she shot her arm up and grabbed what felt like a rope. The rope pulled her, and up and up she went. When she broke through the surface of the lake, her lungs heaved and she gulped in the air, the precious, delicious air.

She coughed and spluttered but got her breath. When her eyes cleared, she realized she wasn't holding a rope at all, she was holding a tail. The body in front of the tail was a dog.

Relentless!

Gratitude burst in her chest. Relentless! She was back!

Relentless licked her face, and Robin grinned. Ari swam towards her with a life jacket and helped her put it on. The two sisters locked eyes and they both smiled at the same time.

A scream split the air.

Robin turned to see Brittany bobbing in her life jacket, the blood draining from her face. Robin swung around and saw the reason for her terror. The mother bear was streaming through the water towards Brittany, her eyes frenzied with anger. She was going to attack.

Without thinking, Robin lunged towards Brittany. The impact plunged them both under the water, but their life jackets buoyed them to the surface again. The bear was just yards away.

Startled by the splashing and commotion, the mother bear stopped her forward motion. She looked at Robin in a confused, questioning way. She sniffed, and picking up Robin's scent, suddenly turned and swam away.

*She remembered*, Robin thought. *She remembered*.

Robin watched as the mother bear led Mukwa away towards the far shore. The rope trailed in the water behind him. Robin smiled. The mother bear's teeth would cut that rope off in seconds once they were on land.

Beside her, Brittany spluttered, "That was the scariest moment of my life." Her teeth were chattering so loud, Robin could hear them.

There was a roar, and Conner appeared beside them on his Jet Ski.

"Idiot!" Ari shouted.

Conner reached out and hauled Brittany back up onto her Jet Ski. Then the two of them charged off.

"Good riddance," Ari said.

Robin felt giddy and breathless all at the same time. Relentless was swimming around her again, so she took hold of her collar. Ari took hold of Robin, and all three of them began swimming back to shore. They were less than halfway across when they were met by their father and Brodie, who were rowing out to help.

"Thank god you're okay," their dad said, pulling one then the other of them into the boat. "We just got back from the pound, and Relentless jumped from the truck and headed for the lake. Now I know why!"

He motioned to Brodie, and the two of them pulled Relentless in. Robin wrapped her arms around her dog and held her close. As she did, she could feel Brodie's warm hand on her back.

"We'll go back for the canoe once we have you two back on shore," Robin's dad said. His eyes went from Robin to Ari and back again. This time he was looking at them both with appreciation and warmth. Like he used to.

Back on land, Zo-Zo threw her arms around Robin. "I thought you were going to die. I called the police, I called an ambulance. I called everyone!"

A siren wailed in the distance, growing louder. The sheriff pulled up in his cruiser. He got out of his car and took a long, slow look at Robin. "Geez, kid, there's never a dull moment around you, is there?"

Conner and Brittany landed their Jet Skis and walked towards the gathering crowd.

Rick Kingshot shoved his way to his children. "You two all right?" he asked.

"They almost drowned Robin," Zo-Zo challenged. She grabbed the sheriff's arm. "Conner was harassing the bears out there, too. That's cruelty to animals!"

"My son wouldn't do something like that," Kingshot said.

"Oh, yes, he would," Zo-Zo shouted. "I saw!"

The sheriff crossed his large arms over his chest. "I don't think a man of Mr. Kingshot's reputation would lie. Would you, Mr. Kingshot?"

Kingshot crossed his arms as well. "I certainly would not."

"*I* saw what Conner did too!" Ari said in that strong, certain way she had when she wanted to sound like she was reciting a law.

The sheriff gave Mr. Kingshot a triumphant look. "Who's going to believe a bunch of kids!"

Zo-Zo held up her camera. "I have all the proof we need. Right here!"

Conner lunged for the camera. In the skirmish, it fell to the ground. Ari dove for it and got it. She pulled it protectively into her chest.

Conner looked at her. "Give me that!"

Ari shook her head solemnly. "No way!"

Conner turned away and strode off. His father followed.

Brittany, her hair wet and bedraggled, watched them leave. Then she raised her eyes to Robin, and the two of them stared at each other for a moment. Finally, she gave Robin a small nod of gratitude and walked away.

# CHAPTER
# TWENTY-THREE

Robin stood on the ladder and held up the other end of the newly painted wooden sign. She tried to make her end the same height as the part her father was holding.

"Is it level?" her dad called to Griff, who was standing back by the gate.

"Up a little at your end, Robin," Griff shouted. "Okay, okay, that's it!"

Her father drove some screws into the wood to secure the sign then helped Robin down. They all stood back to see what it looked like.

Squirm grinned. "Wow."

The sign was a deep forest green and had the words *The Wild Place* embossed in large gold letters.

"Snazzy," Griff said. She turned to Josh, who was standing a few feet away, the small owl perched on his shoulder. "You did a good job."

Josh, who'd been spending a lot of time at the shelter lately, looked pleased. He had made the sign in his shop class. He shot a glance at Ari, who smiled at him easily.

"It's a huge improvement over the cardboard one I put up a while back," Griff said. She patted her son's shoulder. "Guess that makes us the real thing now."

He waved the certificate he'd taken from his pocket. "Yup. We're now a legal wild animal rehabilitation centre."

"I can hardly believe it," Griff said. "I feel like I should pinch myself when everything goes this well. Kind of makes me nervous."

Robin knew what she meant. Lately, it seemed as if nothing could go wrong. Especially now that Ed Goodings had been sworn in as mayor. Not only had he made sure The Wild Place was deemed official, but he'd also managed to wrestle some funds out of the town's budget for its continued existence.

As if that wasn't wonderful enough, Griff had then procured an even larger sum of money from a local philanthropist who loved animals. The Wild Place was now well on its way. They were in the process of upgrading all the enclosures and building a few new ones. And Robin's dad had set up an actual operating room where he could perform surgeries. Sometimes he even asked Robin to scrub up and hand him instruments as he did his work. It amazed Robin to see the insides of an animal. Who would have guessed that each organ would have such a beautiful colour? The lungs were bubble-gum pink, the liver was wet-earth brown, and the heart was red, although it wasn't shaped like she'd imagined. But still, it was incredible to watch it chug blood through an animal's body.

Assisting her father made her think she too might become a vet when she grew up after all, but she was interested in environmental stuff, too, so she wasn't sure. She, Brodie, and Zo-Zo were already trying to think up other eco-games. It thrilled Robin to see the one they'd designed up on the Internet. The three of them liked to go to their site to see how many people had made use of it. So far, over a thousand had. Change was happening, person by person, just as Brodie had said it would.

The phone rang.

"I'll get it," Robin's dad said.

A few minutes later, he came out with his keys. "A doe's got her antlers stuck in a clothesline. I'll be back soon."

"Back to normal," Griff said, waving him off. She picked up the ball and threw it for Einstein. He tore across the yard to get it. Gutsy raced him for it. Einstein got to it first, but Gutsy tried to yank it out of his mouth.

"No, Gutsy! No!" Squirm shouted.

Gutsy was the new name for Greedy Guts. They had given it to her in the hopes that it would be more attractive to prospective owners, as they still needed to find a home for her.

Lately, Robin had found herself not really minding Gutsy so much. Sure, the dog still tried to get her own way, but with fewer dogs around as competition, Gutsy didn't seem to need to push her weight around so much any more.

A few days ago, Brodie had suggested they give Gutsy to Brittany. "She wants a dog. Really wants a dog," he had said.

Robin said she'd think about it, but she knew she was going to agree. She felt sorry for Brittany these days. After people had found out about what had happened on the lake, her dad hadn't done well at the polls and had lost the election. That had to hurt, Robin thought. But then, on top of that, Robin knew that Brittany was being forced to face the fact that Brodie would never be her boyfriend. That was a lot of loss. Robin knew about loss. So, if giving away a puppy would make Brittany feel a bit better, she was going to do it.

Robin felt Griff's arm on hers. "You ready?"

With Relentless trotting happily behind her, Robin followed Griff down to the lake. Squirm came too and threw a stick into the water. Relentless leapt after it, plunging in and causing a huge splash.

"You'll be doing that one day," Griff said. "Jumping into the water."

Robin gave her grandmother a weak smile. Right now she couldn't imagine that. But she trusted Griff, so she put on her lifejacket and fastened the snaps tightly.

"Okay," Griff said. "You know the drill." Robin took Griff's hand. The first time the two of them had gone near the water, all they'd done was sit on the dock and dangle their toes in the lake. They'd done that for days, until Robin was comfortable going further. The next step was putting her feet in the water up to her ankles. The time after that, she'd let the water come up to her knees. Once Robin had "mastered the dock," as Griff had put it, she'd moved Robin to doing the same thing in the lake itself. Lately, Robin had walked so far in, the water had risen to the top of her shoulders.

Now, as the two of them stood on shore, Griff reminded her. "Just take one more step today. One more baby step."

Robin inched forward until the water licked at her chin.

"Every journey, even the longest ones, starts with one tiny step," Griff said. A moment later she asked, "You scared yet?"

"Just starting."

"Don't go any further. You know what to do. Just breathe until you aren't afraid any more."

Robin had thought that after paddling the canoe, she would no longer be afraid of the water, but that wasn't true. But now she knew she could face her fear. And to her surprise, no matter how scared she was at the beginning of these "swimming lessons," her fear always seemed to get tired of itself and ease up within a few minutes. It helped that Griff stayed with her until it did.

At the end of the "lesson," Griff, as usual, asked her if she wanted "a float."

Robin nodded, and they walked back to where it was very shallow. Griff took three foam noodles and put them under Robin's legs, waist, and neck. Sitting down in the water herself, Griff then eased Robin into her arms so that Robin was floating on her back. When Robin had first tried this, she'd found it almost impossible to let go and trust that she wasn't going to sink, but now that she'd done it so many times, it was easier.

As she lay back, the waves rocked her in a gentle, rhythmic way. Above her, some white, fluffy clouds billowed across the sky. Close by, she could hear the ebb and flow of the water as it lapped against the shore. She moved her arms like fins and began to move along the shallow water of the shore.

Griff walked along beside her, grinning. "You're swimming, my girl, swimming!"

Relentless paddled up to her side, wiggling with happiness. Robin looked into Relentless's eyes. They weren't the same colour, but they reminded Robin of her mother anyway. Of the steady love her mother always had for her.

After the funeral, Robin had felt certain she'd lost that love forever, but lately she'd realized it was still there, wrapped around her like a warm but firm hug that never went away. Sometimes she felt it so strongly, so vividly, she could have sworn that her mother was actually there, holding her. And who knows, maybe she *was* there. Just not visible. Like Griff said. It certainly felt like she was.

This realization felt incredibly freeing. It meant that no matter what she was doing, hanging out with friends or helping hurt animals, she had something warm and protective to rely on. She felt safe. Safe to have all the adventures she wanted. And she did want adventures. Lots of them.

# ACKNOWLEDGEMENTS

For writerly contributions, thank you to Craig Rintoul, Theresa Sansome, Cheryl Cooper, Cathy Kuntz, Martin Avery, Cornerstone Literary Agency, and Syd Field.

For support in every way, thank you to Jason Caddy, Rod Govan, Caroline Robertson, Linda Wright, Liz Gilbert, Vicki Govan, Gaile Hood, Kate Oldham, and Brian Stuart. Deep appreciation to Serene Chazan and Theresa Sansome for reminding me to honour the truest parts of me.

Heartfelt gratitude to Audrey Tournay at the Aspen Valley Wildlife Sanctuary for all her help and great work.

Special thanks to Allister Thompson for his thorough and inspired editing and Sylvia McConnell for being the gutsy, believing publisher that she is.

# MORE GREAT FICTION FOR YOUNG READERS

**True Colours**
by Lucy Lemay Cellucci
9781926607139
$9.95

Fifteen-year-old Zoe is many things, but confident is not one of them. Perhaps that's why she prefers the company of animals. A self-professed advocate for their rights, Zoe is not above taking matters into her own hands. But the stakes are raised when she finds herself at the centre of a dangerous conspiracy involving the disappearance of animals from a shelter. She turns to street-savvy Alex Fisher, her troubled Social Studies partner, to help unravel the mystery. Zoe soon learns that nothing is as it appears, as she is confronted by angry parents, a dangerous sociopath, and an ill-advised romance.

Rosa Jordan

**Wild Spirits**
by Rosa Jordan
9781554887293
$12.99

Eleven-year-old Danny Ryan and nineteen-year-old Wendy Marshall think their friendship is only about looking after two baby raccoons that Danny has rescued. But when a bank holdup upsets Wendy so much that she can hardly stand to be around people, she leaves her job as a teller, retreats to a farm, and surrounds herself with injured and orphaned wildlife. Danny, neglected at home and considered weird in a town where other boys are into hunting, finds peace on the farm, too, plus excitement, as he and Wendy adopt ever more exotic animals such as llamas, bobcats, a serval, an ocelot, and a blind lynx.

Over time the two friends develop a bond that goes beyond care of the animals to caring for each other. As it turns out, Wendy rescues not just wildlife but Danny, as well. What's more, the bank robbers are still at large and still a threat, and Danny, now fourteen, must act to save Wendy's life.

**Jak's Story**
by Aaron Bell
9781554887101
$10.99

Thirteen-year-old Jak Loren is a typical boy with the usual problems a family with older sisters and younger brothers presents. Never mind the troubles at school — bullies and girls!

When Jak goes to the ravine near his home in Brantford to get away from Steven Burke, a bully who's been tormenting him, he discovers the ravine has a history that's much older than he thought. He meets Grandfather Rock, who shares with him the story of the people who have lived near the ravine for thousands of years. Soon Jak's eyes are opened to a new world of beings and respect.

He learns about First Nations people and how their teachings inhabit the spirits of all living things that surround us even today. The tales of the First Nations help Jak to understand that the gift of life is something to be cherished. And when a construction crew arrives in his neighbourhood and threatens his beloved ravine, Jak knows he has to act to save it.

**Snakes and Ladders**
by Shaun Smith
9781550028409
$12.99

For as long as thirteen-year-old Paige Morrow can remember, the tree fort in the giant oak near her cottage in Ontario's Muskoka has been her sanctuary. Now everything is changing. It's the summer of 1971, and she and her little brother, Toby, have been at their cottage with their mother since school let out. But this year, Paige feels more alone than ever. Her father has stopped coming up from the city on weekends, while her mother buries herself in whiskey and writing.

Paige retreats to her tree fort, but becomes concerned when the farmer who owns the property hires a creepy arborist — a "tree doctor." Is something wrong with the farm's apple orchard or with her tree? When Paige befriends the arborist's troubled teenage daughter, Janine, and her group of rowdy locals, she is pulled into a maze of dark secrets and shocking truths that leads to a life-and-death confrontation.

Available at your favourite bookseller.

**DUNDURN**
www.dundurn.com

What did you think of this book?
Visit **www.dundurn.com**
for reviews, videos, updates, and more!